QUIET TIME

Fargo pointed his Colt. "I'll put you out of your misery."

"No!" Lector cried, his eyes going wide. "Let me go natural."

"Don't blubber then," Fargo said.

"Damn, you are hard."

Fargo squatted and wiped the toothpick clean on Lector's pants.

"Fletch was right about you. You are more dangerous than most."

"I'm still breathing," Fargo said.

"Fletcher should have shot you right off."

Fargo finished wiping and slid the toothpick into his ankle sheath. "As robbers you'd make good store clerks."

"First you kill me and now you insult me."

"Hush up and die," Fargo said.

"I will not," Lector said. "I deserve to say my piece. These are my last moments and I'm entitled."

"Nothing says I have to listen."

"You've already gutted me like a fish. What else can you do?"

"This," Fargo said, and shot him between the eyes.

THE
TRAILSMAN
#378

WYOMING
WINTERKILL

by

Jon Sharpe

A SIGNET BOOK

SIGNET
Published by the Penguin Group
Penguin Group (USA) Inc., 375 Hudson Street,
New York, New York 10014, USA

USA / Canada / UK / Ireland / Australia / New Zealand / India / South Africa / China

Penguin Books Ltd., Registered Offices: 80 Strand, London WC2R 0RL, England
For more information about the Penguin Group visit penguin.com.

First published by Signet, an imprint of New American Library,
a division of Penguin Group (USA) Inc.

First Printing, April 2013

The first chapter of this book previously appeared in *Bounty Hunt*, the three hundred
seventy-seventh volume in this volume.

 REGISTERED TRADEMARK—MARCA REGISTRADA

ISBN 978-0-451-41575-2

Printed in the United States of America
10 9 8 7 6 5 4 3 2 1

PUBLISHER'S NOTE
This is a work of fiction. Names, characters, places, and incidents either are the
product of the author's imagination or are used fictitiously, and any resemblance to
actual persons, living or dead, business establishments, events, or locales is entirely
coincidental.

The publisher does not have any control over and does not assume any responsi-
bility for author or third-party Web sites or their content.

The Trailsman

Beginnings . . . they bend the tree and they mark the man. Skye Fargo was born when he was eighteen. Terror was his midwife, vengeance his first cry. Killing spawned Skye Fargo, ruthless, cold-blooded murder. Out of the acrid smoke of gunpowder still hanging in the air, he rose, cried out a promise never forgotten.

The Trailsman they began to call him all across the West: searcher, scout, hunter, the man who could see where others only looked, his skills for hire but not his soul, the man who lived each day to the fullest, yet trailed each tomorrow. Skye Fargo, the Trailsman, the seeker who could take the wildness of a land and the wanting of a woman and make them his own.

The Rocky Mountains in the winter, 1861—
where the cold and snow . . . and hot lead . . .
made for an early grave.

1

Wyoming in the winter wasn't for the faint of heart.

Once it turned cold, it stayed cold. Not the kind of cold back east, where a man could throw on a heavy coat and forget about it. This was a biting cold that froze the marrow. The wind made it worse. The temperature might be ten degrees; the wind made it seem like it was fifty below.

Skye Fargo supposed he should be used to it. He'd been through Wyoming enough times. But even bundled as he was in a heavy bearskin coat over his buckskins, he was cold as hell.

He'd tied his bandanna over his hat and knotted it under his chin so the wind couldn't whip it from his head. He could see his breath and the Ovaro's. Each inhale seared his lungs with ice so that the simple act of breathing hurt.

Given his druthers, Fargo would rather be anywhere than where he was. But he'd signed on to scout for the army for a spell and the army wanted him to go to Fort Laramie. By his best reckoning he was five days out.

The sky was an ominous gray. Thick clouds pregnant with the promise of snow had yet to unleash their burden.

A winter storm was brewing, and if Fargo was any judge, it would be a bitch.

He hadn't stuck to the main trail. He wanted to get to the fort as quickly as he could, so he was cutting overland.

He came to a tributary of the Platte and a crossing he

remembered, and drew rein in surprise. He didn't remember a trading post being there. Yet one was on the other side, a long, low building with a crude sign that proclaimed it was run by one George Wilbur and he paid top prices for prime plews. At the bottom, in small letters, it mentioned simply WHISKEY.

Fargo had no great hankering to stop. But half a bottle would warm his innards and ward off the cold for a while when he resumed his ride.

Three horses were at the hitch rail. They looked miserable and he didn't blame them. Only a poor excuse for a human being would leave his animal out in the cold. Especially when around to the side was a lean-to. He dismounted and led the stallion in out of the worst of the wind.

Rubbing his hands, Fargo breathed on his fingers to warm them. When he had some feeling, he shucked his Henry from the saddle scabbard, cradled it in the crook of his left elbow, and walked around to the front door. Before he entered he opened his bearskin coat and slid his right hand under and rested it on his Colt.

The rawhide hinges protested with loud creaks.

Welcome warmth washed over him. A fire blazed in a stone fireplace, a pile of wood heaped high beside it.

At the moment a woman of thirty or so was bent over, adding some. She looked around.

So did everyone else.

The place was about what Fargo expected. Log walls, the chinks filled with clay. Rafters overhead. A bar and four tables.

Three men were playing cards; the owners of the horses at the hitch rail, Fargo guessed.

Behind the bar a man in an apron was wiping glasses. He had thick sideburns and a bristly mustache and dark eyes that glittered.

For Fargo, it was distrust at first sight.

The three men didn't inspire brotherly love, either. They were unkempt, their clothes shabby, their coats not much better. Their eyes glittered, too, like wolves sizing up prey.

But Fargo wanted that drink. He crossed to the bar and set the Henry down with a loud thunk and swept his coat clear of his holster.

"How do, mister," the barman said. "Cold, ain't it?"

"A bottle," Fargo said. "Monongahela."

"Sure thing." The man turned to a shelf lined with bottles and picked one that hadn't been opened. "I'm George Wilbur, by the way."

"Good for you."

Wilbur opened the bottle and set it down.

As Fargo reached for it he caught his reflection in a dusty mirror. His beard needed a trim and his blue eyes had a piercing intensity that he was told made some uncomfortable. He raised the bottle, admired the amber liquor, and took a long swallow that burned warmth clear to his toes.

"I don't water mine down, like some do," Wilbur boasted.

Fargo grunted. He undid his bandanna and retied it around his neck. The bottle in one hand and his Henry in the other, he walked over to the fireplace, helping himself to a chair from a table and pushing it with his boot as he went. He sat so he was partly facing the fire and could keep an eye on the rest of the room's occupants. Leaning his rifle against the chair, he placed the bottle in his lap and held his hands out to the flames.

The woman added another log. She had brown hair and a pear-shaped face that wouldn't be so plain if she gussied up. Her homespun dress couldn't hide her ample bosom and long legs. She gave him a nice smile and turned away.

George Wilbur came over. "Don't say much, do you, friend?"

3

"Not in this life or any other," Fargo said.

"Eh?"

"Are we friends?"

"Oh," Wilbur said. He shifted his weight from one leg to the other. "I'm just making small talk."

Fargo looked at him.

Wilbur gestured. "We don't get many folks stopping by, is all."

"Makes this a damn stupid spot to build a trading post."

"I make enough to get by and that's what counts," Wilbur said.

Fargo treated himself to another swallow.

"We've got eats if you're hungry," Wilbur said. "The woman here will cook for you. Fifty cents, and all you can eat."

When Fargo didn't say anything, Wilbur coughed and turned and went back behind the bar.

The woman was poking through the wood box. Without looking at him she said quietly, "I'm not a bad cook if I say so myself."

Fargo took another chug.

"My husband, Clyde, got knifed by an Injun when he went out to use the privy and I sort of got stuck here."

"A war party attacked the trading post?" Fargo asked out of mild interest.

"No," the woman said. "There was just the one redskin."

"Only one?"

The woman nodded at the three men playing cards. "That's what they said. One of them is a tracker. He showed me a few scrape marks and told me they were moccasin tracks."

About to take another swallow, Fargo paused with the bottle half tilted. "When was this?"

"Oh, it must have been three weeks ago, or better. About the time the weather turned cold."

"Hell," Fargo said.

The woman turned. "Something the matter?"

"What's your handle?"

"My what?"

"Your name," Fargo said. "And where are you from?"

"Oh. My name is Margaret. Margaret Atwood. I'm from Ohio. My husband and I were on our way to Oregon Country and we got separated from the wagon train and were pretty much lost when we found this place, thank goodness."

"I didn't see a wagon when I rode up."

"Oh. Mr. Wilbur sold it. Seeing as how Clyde was dead, I didn't want to go on to Oregon by my lonesome. So he was kind enough to find a buyer and give me half the money."

"Half?"

"Well, he had to go to a lot of bother. His friends there had to ride to the Oregon Trail and wait for the next wagon train to come along and ask if anyone wanted to buy ours and when no one did they had to wait around for the next."

"Mr. Wilbur was damned generous."

"That's what he said." Margaret grew sad and bowed her head. "I didn't much care, to tell you the truth. With Clyde gone life didn't hardly seem worth living."

Fargo glanced at Wilbur, polishing glasses again, and at the three wolves playing cards. "Son of a bitch."

"Is it me or do you cuss a lot?"

"How many others have stopped here since you came?" Fargo asked.

Margaret knit her brow. "Let me see. There was that traveling parson on his mule. And a drummer. And another wagon with an older couple. They were lost, and Mr. Fletcher"—she pointed at the tallest of the card players—"he's the tracker. He offered to guide them to Fort Laramie. He and his friends were gone about two days."

5

"Hell," Fargo said. He told himself it was none of his affair. He didn't know the old couple and he didn't know her.

"Their granddaughter was the sweetest little girl," Margaret remarked.

"How's that again?"

"The old couple. They had their granddaughter with them. Jessie, her name was. Her folks got killed in a fire and her grandparents were taking her to live with an uncle who'd settled in the Willamette Valley."

"How old?"

"Jessie? She was ten."

The whiskey in Fargo's gut turned bitter.

"Why do you look as if you want to bite someone's head off?"

"Did I hear something about food?"

"Venison," Margaret said with a bob of her chin. "Fletcher shot a buck this morning, so the meat is as fresh as can be. I'll whip up potatoes and there are carrots in the root cellar. Would that do?"

"Throw in coffee and you have a deal."

Margaret brightened and stood. "That's fine. And you help me in the bargain."

"I do?"

"Wilbur gives me five cents for every meal I cook for him."

"That much?"

"He's a kind man."

"It's good you're happy," Fargo said.

"I'm lucky to have the work," Margaret replied. "Now you stay put. It shouldn't take me more than twenty minutes or so."

"No hurry," Fargo said. He had some prodding to do first, and it might end in gunplay.

2

His bottle in one hand and the thumb of his other hooked in his gun belt, Fargo strode over to the table where the three wolves were playing cards.

Fletcher, the tall one, wore a perpetual sneer, courtesy of a scar at the corner of his mouth. He had on a faded wool coat and a hat with a split in the brim. "What do you want?"

"Thought I might sit in." Fargo pulled his poke out. "If you're tired of playing for toothpicks." He'd noticed that they were, in fact, using toothpicks instead of money or chips.

Fletcher and his friends swapped glances of pure greed. The other two were enough alike to be brothers; both were short and stocky with faces that hinted at cruel natures.

All three wore six-shooters on their hips.

"Have a seat, friend," Fletcher said, indicating an empty chair. "We'll be happy to take your money."

Fargo eased down and leaned the Henry against his left leg. He placed his poke on the table.

"Where might you be headed?" asked one of the brothers.

"Fort Laramie," Fargo saw no harm in revealing as he loosened the drawstring to his poke.

"Taking the Oregon Trail to the Pacific, are you?" asked the other.

"I'm a scout."

Fletcher's fingers froze in the act of shuffling. "You work for the army?"

The brothers both stiffened slightly.

"At the moment," Fargo said.

"They must be expecting you," Fletcher remarked as he riffled the cards.

"I suppose they are," Fargo said, "since Colonel Harrington sent for me."

"Ah," Fletcher said, and gave the other two a pointed look. "Then you'll be going on your way after we're done here."

"He will?" the brother on the right said.

"He will," Fletcher said.

Fargo almost laughed in scorn. They were so obvious, they might as well wear a sign like the one out front.

"This here is Lector," Fletcher said, gesturing at the brother on the right. "And this here is Hector," he said, introducing the other one.

"We didn't catch your name," Lector said.

"I didn't give it," Fargo said.

"Is it me," Hector said, "or are you a mite prickly?"

"More than a mite," Fargo replied.

"I don't know as I like that," Hector said.

"One of us doesn't give a damn what you like."

Hector flushed with anger and put his hands flat on the table as if he was about to rise.

"Now, now," Fletcher said. "This is a friendly game. Hector, you be civil—you hear me?"

Hector muttered something.

"I mean it. This gent works for the *army*. You understand me? He doesn't show up at the fort, they might wonder why."

"And send a patrol to look for him," Lector said.

"Exactly." Fletcher smiled at Fargo. "You have to forgive Hector. He's prickly, too."

Fargo bided his time. He let three hands go by. It was his turn to deal and he was sliding cards to each of them when he asked, "Did you burn the wagon or just leave it?"

Fletcher looked up so sharply, it was a wonder he didn't snap his neck. "What was that?"

"The wagon with the old couple and their grand-daughter," Fargo said. "Did you burn it after you robbed them?"

"Mister," Fletcher said, "I don't know what in hell you're talking about."

"It takes five days to reach the fort from here on horse-back when the weather is good," Fargo said. "Ten to twelve in a heavy Conestoga."

"So?"

"So I hear tell you offered to guide them but came back in two days."

Lector squirmed in his chair. Hector commenced to chew on his lip.

Fletcher, though, was shrewder than both of them put together. "And you think we did them in because of that?" He laughed. "Jesus, what do you take us for?"

"Killers," Fargo said.

Fletcher laughed louder. "Will you listen to yourself? For your information, mister, they only needed us to point them in the right direction. Not to take them the whole way."

"That's right," Lector said, bobbing his head.

"We only had to point the way," Hector chimed in.

"I can't say I think much of you accusing us," Fletcher said.

Fargo shrugged. "My mistake."

"You don't know us," Lector said.

"Who do you think you are?" Hector demanded.

"Jacks or better to open, wasn't it?" Fargo said, and pushed a coin to the middle of the table. "It will cost you a dollar to stay in."

Fletcher had set his cards down and was tapping a finger on them. "We don't want you spreading stories about us."

"I'll ask around when I get to the fort. Likely as not someone will recollect the old couple."

Lector and Hector shot anxious glances at Fletcher, who smiled and said, "A lot of wagons stop at the fort. There's no reason anyone should remember just the one."

"Colonel Harrington will," Fargo said. "He has a girl about their granddaughter's age." Which was a bald-faced lie.

"Good," Fletcher said. "Then you'll know we weren't up to no good."

"You'll know," Lector declared.

Fargo dropped it and went on playing. He'd planted a seed. Now he had to watch his back every second. It amused him, the glares they threw his way when they thought he wasn't looking. He played until Margaret came out of the back bearing a tray laden with food; then he bowed out and went over to the corner table.

A thick slab of venison made his mouth water. True to her word, she'd prepared potatoes with gravy and chopped carrots and three slices of buttered bread. Add a fresh pot of coffee, and he was in hog heaven. He ate with relish.

He noticed that the three wolves kept glancing over. They weren't happy.

At one point, Fletcher got up and went to the bar and paid for a bottle. As he paid, he leaned in and said something to George Wilbur that made Wilbur look over at the corner in alarm.

Fargo had wondered if all four were in on it. Now he knew.

He finished his meal, dipping the last of the bread in the last of the gravy. Pushing the plate away, he sat back, patted his gut in contentment, and poured another cup of coffee.

Margaret came out of the back. "All cleaned up," she said with a smile. "Did you like it?"

"You're a damn fine cook."

"My Clyde used to think so too. I thank you."

Fargo pushed a chair out with his foot. "Have a seat if you'd like."

Margaret glanced at the bar. "I probably shouldn't. Mr. Wilbur doesn't like it when I talk too much to people who stop by."

"Who cares what he likes? He's not your husband."

"He sure acts like he is sometimes. Between you and me, I think he wants to be after I get done mourning for Clyde." Margaret squared her slim shoulders. "By God, I want to talk to you and I will, and he can go to the devil."

"That's the spirit." Fargo poured some whiskey into his coffee and wagged the bottle at her. "Care for a drink?"

"Oh my, no. I've only ever touched spirits two or three times in my whole life and never liked it much. It's too bitter tasting."

"You get used to it." Fargo saw Wilbur staring. He rested his forearms on the table and gave her his most charming smile. "You don't have to stay here if you don't want to."

"What are you saying?"

"That I'll take you with me when I leave. As far as Fort Laramie. From there you can head back east or do whatever you want."

"I'd like to go back to Ohio but it will take me a while to save up the money."

"You told me that Wilbur gave you half the money from the sale of your wagon," Fargo recalled.

"He did, yes, but he didn't get anywhere near what it was worth. My half came to barely two hundred dollars."

"Hell," Fargo said, and drank straight from the bottle. "Did you ever think he might be cheating you?"

"It occurred to me, yes," Margaret said. "But he's so nice, and all. And most people don't do things like that to one another. Not where I was raised."

"This isn't Ohio."

"I understand that. I'm not naive. But he's been so kind about everything. It wasn't his fault that Indian killed my Clyde."

"Unless it wasn't an Indian."

Margaret gave a mild start. "What are you implying?"

"You know damn well what I mean."

"Surely not." Margaret shook her head. "No. I refuse to believe that. No one could be that despicable."

"What if I can prove it?"

"How?"

"Do you have a room of your own?"

"A small one, yes, but I don't see—"

"Take me into the back with you," Fargo proposed. "We'll see what Wilbur does."

"He's bound to think that you and I—" Margaret couldn't bring herself to finish. "It might provoke him something awful."

"Good."

"I don't know," Margaret said with a quick look at the bar. "After he's been so nice—"

"Nice, hell," Fargo said. "If I'm right, he and his friends murdered your husband to take everything you own and keep you here."

"Surely not."

"How about we find out?" Fargo placed his hand on hers.

"I don't know," Margaret said again. "It might make him mad. What if he becomes violent?"

Fargo smiled. "I hope to hell he does."

3

George Wilbur came from behind the bar with a towel over his shoulder and his fists balled. Striding over, he angrily snapped, "No touching, mister."

Fargo, his hand still on Margaret's, let his smile widen. "No touching what?"

"Not what, who," Wilbur growled, with a nod at Margaret. "No touching her. You pay for a drink and food, not the other."

"She your missus?" Fargo asked.

Wilbur went from mad to flustered. "Well, no."

"Your sister?"

"No, of course not."

"Your mother?"

"Damn it to hell, you know she's not," Wilbur said. "Quit asking stupid questions."

"If she's not any of those," Fargo said, "then you don't have a say."

"She works here," Wilbur declared.

"Not anymore."

"What?"

Margaret opened her mouth as if to say the same thing but caught herself.

"She's leaving with me," Fargo said.

Wilbur sputtered and glanced toward his three friends and then blurted, "She can't. I mean, I took her on out of the goodness of my heart with the understanding that she'd work here more than a few weeks."

"She's a grown woman. She can do whatever the hell she wants." Fargo stood and pulled Margaret to her feet. "I'll go with you and help you pack. Lead the way." He grabbed the whiskey bottle and shoved it in one of the deep pockets of his bearskin coat.

George Wilbur looked fit to bust a gut. He reluctantly moved aside, saying to her, "I wish you wouldn't."

"My room is in the back," Margaret said to Fargo.

The narrow hall opened into the kitchen and another room, where Wilbur lived. Hers was so small that Fargo could spread his arms and his fingertips almost brushed the opposite walls. There was a bed and a tiny table and that was it.

Her carpetbag was under the bed. Pulling it out, Margaret opened it and began to fold a cotton robe she'd left lying on the bed. "I don't know why I'm doing this. But I sense I can trust you."

Fargo had left the door open a crack. Taking his hat off, he peered out.

Wilbur and Fletcher were at the far end of the hall. Fletcher looked angry as hell. Suddenly Fletcher gripped the front of Wilbur's apron and put a hand on his revolver and Wilbur blanched and vigorously bobbed his head.

"What do you see?" Margaret asked.

"My seed has taken root."

Margaret placed her robe in the carpetbag. "Is that a good thing or a bad thing?"

Putting his hat back on, Fargo clasped her hands in his and sat her on the bed. "Listen. They can't let us leave. They won't risk you telling anyone about your husband and that old couple."

"I still can't believe they're as wicked as you make them out to be."

"The proof will be when they try to stop us from reaching the front door."

"Stop us how?"

Fargo stared.

"Oh," Margaret said. "Can't we avoid that? I don't want bloodshed."

"It will be them or us."

"No," Margaret said. "There has to be another way." Her face lit with an idea. "I have it. We'll go out the back and sneak around to your horse. I don't have one of my own, so I'm afraid we'll have to ride double."

Fargo would rather confront the four men and get it over with, and said so.

"Please. Let's do this my way. I couldn't live with myself if blood was spilled on my account."

Fargo scowled. He could take her out the front anyway but she might give him a hard time and he needed to concentrate on Fletcher and his friends.

"I'm begging you," Margaret said.

Fargo gave in. "We'll do it your way."

"Thank you," Margaret said, and pecked him on the cheek.

Fargo checked the hall. Fletcher and Wilbur weren't there. Crooking a finger, he said, "Let's skedaddle."

A heavy coat hung on a hook on the wall. Margaret took it down, shrugged into it, and held her carpetbag to her bosom. "I'm ready."

Fargo stepped out and she slipped by. A blast of cold air hit them as he opened the back door.

Levering a round into the Henry's chamber, Fargo moved to the corner.

"You shouldn't need to use that," Margaret said.

Fargo led her to the lean-to. He untied the Ovaro's reins and brought the stallion out and turned to give Margaret a boost.

"Did you hear something?" she whispered as she settled behind the saddle.

The Ovaro raised its head and pricked its ears.

Fargo saw Lector running toward the lean-to with a pistol in his hand. Lector was looking at her and the Ovaro but apparently hadn't spotted him. Stepping out, Fargo slammed the Henry's stock against Lector's head and Lector folded and pitched forward.

"Goodness," Margaret gasped. "Was that really necessary?"

Fargo quickly climbed on. He shoved the Henry into the scabbard, reined around, and resorted to his spurs.

They were past the trading post and almost to the brush when a shout blasted. Someone had found Lector and was yelling. It sounded like Hector.

Fargo felt Margaret's arm loop around his waist and squeeze tight. He went about a hundred yards at a gallop, then reined to the northwest and rode at a trot for a while. By then he was half a mile from the trading post and didn't see anyone after them.

"I think we did it."

"And no blood was spilled," Margaret crowed. "Thank you for trying my way instead of yours."

"It's your conscience."

"How do you mean?"

"If I'm right, you and your husband and that old couple weren't the first folks they've killed and robbed. And you won't be the last. They'll keep at it until someone plants them."

"I hadn't thought of that," Margaret said quietly. "Anyone they harm in the future, it's on my shoulders, isn't it?"

Fargo grunted.

"I don't like that notion," Margaret said. "What can I do?"

"File a report at Fort Laramie."

"What can the army do? It's a civilian matter."

"I'll see that Colonel Harrington gets word to a federal marshal," Fargo said. It was the best he could do since she wouldn't let him do what he should.

"I'm glad that's settled." Margaret shivered and pressed against him. "Mercy me, it's cold. And that wind."

Fargo had slowed to a walk. Since no one was after them, he saw no reason to ride the Ovaro into the ground.

The sun slowly climbed in the cloudless pale sky. The later it grew, the more the wind picked up. Occasional gusts whipped the pines and the cottonwoods.

"I'm freezing," Margaret said.

So was Fargo. He had an eye out for a likely spot to camp. It had to be out of the wind, and where their fire wouldn't be seen from afar.

He considered a stand of saplings, a dry wash, a ring of boulders.

The sun was low on the horizon when he spied a bluff. It wasn't all that high or big but it blocked most of the wind. He drew rein midway along the east side where a cluster of trees had sprung up and sparse grass grew.

Fargo dismounted and helped Margaret down. They both moved stiffly, their limbs half frozen. It was only after he'd gathered firewood and had a small blaze crackling that he began to feel like his usual self.

Margaret held her hands to the fire and did more shivering. "I don't know as I'll ever warm up."

Fargo opened his saddlebags and took out a bundle of pemmican. He offered some to her and she looked at it as if she'd never seen it before.

"What's this?"

"Buff meat ground to a powder and mixed with fat and chokecherries."

Margaret scrunched up her face. "It doesn't sound very appetizing."

"Go hungry then."

She nibbled and, after a few chews, smiled and took a bigger bite. "I was wrong. It's delicious. Did you invent it?"

Fargo chuckled. "Hell, no. Indians did. A lot of tribes eat it. I learned about it from the time I was with the Sioux."

Margaret stopped chewing. "You've lived with redskins?"

"You make them sound like a disease."

"No, no, it's just that—" Margaret stopped. "I don't know what it is, really. Most people don't have a high opinion of them."

"Most whites," Fargo amended.

Margaret digested that, and the piece of pemmican, and asked, "So, do you consider yourself mostly white or mostly red?"

"I consider myself mostly me."

"That's no answer," Margaret said. "But I guess it really doesn't matter, does it?"

"Not one damn bit."

Fargo had stripped his saddle and placed it close to the bluff. Now he did the same with his bedroll, spreading his blankets so the saddle served as a pillow of sorts. "I don't have a spare," he mentioned.

Margaret looked and her cheeks grew pink. "You're not suggesting we share?"

"If it was summer I'd sleep on the ground," Fargo said. But he wasn't about to do it with the ground as cold as ice.

"You *are* suggesting it?"

"Afraid you can't control yourself?" Fargo joked.

"It's not—" Margaret stopped, and swallowed. "I'm perfectly able to control any and all carnal urges, thank you very much."

Fargo pulled down the top blanket and patted it.

"What about you?" Margaret asked. "Can you control your baser nature?"

"I reckon I could if I wanted to," Fargo said, and grinned. "But I never want to."

"Oh my," Margaret said.

4

Fargo honestly tried to get to sleep.

He lay on his side facing the fire, his back to Margaret Atwood. Between the heat of the flames, his bearskin coat, the blankets, and the warmth Margaret's body gave off, he was downright hot.

As soon as the fire went out, he'd cool down and would be comfortable enough that he should get a good night's rest.

Margaret was between him and the bluff. Nothing could get at her unless they went through him. She was on her side, her back to him, the blanket pulled clear to her chin.

She wouldn't stop fidgeting. She rolled onto her back. She rolled onto her side. She rolled back onto her back. Finally she let out the world's longest sigh and whispered, "Are you awake?"

On the verge of dozing off, Fargo roused to drowsily say, "I wouldn't have been in a bit."

"Sorry."

Fargo made himself a little more comfortable and was again about to slip under when she squirmed and uttered another sigh.

"Is it just me or are you roasting?"

"It's not just you."

"I'm sweating like a pig."

Fargo imagined a sheen of perspiration covering her body and felt himself stir, low down.

"Aren't you?"

"I try not to think about it."

"Me too. But I can't stop."

Fargo heard her roll over yet again. He figured she had rolled toward the bluff. She hadn't. A hand found his shoulder and slid along it to his neck. "That tickles," he said. Actually it didn't.

"I used to sleep like this with Clyde," Margaret said. "He never minded."

"Did you sleep with a nightgown on or naked?" Fargo teased, not expecting an answer.

It was all of ten seconds before she softly replied, "I liked to sleep naked."

Well, now, Fargo thought. It was his turn to roll over, toward her. He wound up with his face inches from hers. So close, he felt her breath on his cheek. "This is cozy."

"It is," Margaret said softly.

"I wouldn't want to keep you awake," Fargo said, testing the waters. "We have a long ride ahead of us tomorrow."

"You're not."

Fargo lay there, and when she didn't say or do anything, he closed his eyes and emptied his head and waited for sleep to claim him. It didn't.

"You know," Margaret whispered, "this is downright intimate."

"Hadn't noticed," Fargo lied.

"You give off a lot of heat."

"It's the fire," Fargo said.

Margaret had a nice laugh. "I suppose I should feel uncomfortable lying this close to a man I hardly know, but I don't. Isn't that scandalous?"

"Not from where I lie."

She laughed again, a light, throaty purr that tingled his ears. "You're trying to set me at ease, aren't you?"

"I don't care if you are or you aren't. We need to get some rest."

"That's all right," Margaret said. "You don't need to pretend with me."

Fargo didn't say anything.

"It's normal. It's natural. You being a man and me being a woman."

Fargo opened his eyes. The whites of hers glistened in the firelight. "Noticed that, did you?"

"How could a gal not notice someone as handsome as you? Clyde was downright ugly compared to you." She quickly added, "May his soul rest in peace."

Fargo waited.

"Clyde and I used to do something that always helped me get to sleep."

"He gave you a back rub?"

Margaret's teeth were white in the darkness. "He rubbed a lot more than that."

"You don't say." Fargo shifted his right hand from his hip to the space between his chest and her bosom.

Margaret was quiet a short while. Then, "Do you think you would want to?"

"I'm male."

"And men are always hungry for women? Is that how it goes?"

"So they say," Fargo replied. "I don't have a lot of experience at it." For that whopper, it was a wonder the sky didn't open and a bolt of lightning didn't char him to a cinder.

"It would help me sleep."

Fargo didn't have to be nudged any further. He slid his hand inside her coat and cupped a breast through her dress and heard her gasp.

"Oh my."

"You wanted me to," Fargo said, his throat constricting.

"Yes, I certainly did."

To hell with it, Fargo thought. Sliding his other arm under and around her, he pulled her close and covered her mouth with his. Her lips were deliciously soft, her tongue delightfully wet. Their first kiss went on a good long while and when they eventually parted, she was breathing a lot heavier.

"That was nice. You're a good kisser."

Fargo hoped she wasn't a talker. They were a peeve of his. When a woman made love she should have the sense to shut up and do it, not talk a man to death.

"How am I?" Margaret asked.

"Like sweet candy," Fargo said, and to shut her up, he kissed her again.

Margaret slid so her legs were against his and put her hand on his thigh.

Fargo wasn't expecting what she did next: she moved her hand to his bulge. For a few seconds he thought he'd explode then and there.

"Oh my," Margaret breathed, pulling back. "You're a big one."

Fargo growled deep in his throat.

"A very big one."

"Do me a favor and don't chatter," Fargo requested.

"Do me a favor and let's see if we can do it with our clothes on."

They could.

It took some doing. Fargo had to undo a lot of buttons to get his hand inside her dress but it was worth the trouble. She had marvelously full and surprisingly firm breasts, breasts of a woman half her age. When he pinched and pulled a nipple, she arched her back and moaned.

Margaret moaned louder when he caressed her thighs. She liked that, liked it a lot, liked it so much that when he had been at it a bit, stoking the furnace, as he liked to think of it, she suddenly reached down, gripped his hand, and slid it between her legs.

"What are you waiting for?"

Fargo could take a hint. He parted her nether lips and

she shivered, but not from the cold. She was moist and hot, and when he inserted a finger, she tried to climb inside of him. Her breath was a fire; her melons were molten.

Swift strokes primed her pump. She was bursting with desire. As he eased her onto her back and positioned himself between her legs, she whispered, "Yes. Oh, yes."

Placing the tip of his pole to her velvet sheath, Fargo penetrated her inch by slow inch. She shook and groaned and gripped his shoulders. When he was all the way in he held himself still, savoring the sensation.

"I want you," Margaret said, and fused their mouths.

Fargo commenced to rock. She met each thrust with a sweep of her pelvis. The intensity built. They went at it faster and harder and faster and harder until Margaret gasped and threw back her head and opened her mouth wide in a silent scream of release.

Fargo went on rocking.

Margaret coasted down from whatever heights she had reached, and realized he hadn't stopped. "How can you—?" She sucked in a breath and said, "Oh my. Oh my, oh my, oh my, my, my."

Fargo held off for as long as he could, until there came the moment when his body wouldn't be denied. He exploded with a violence that surprised even him, lifting her half off the ground in his ardor.

Afterward, he gradually slowed and lay panting on top of her.

"You're awful heavy," Margaret said.

Fargo slid onto his side. He managed to pull his buckskins together and closed his leaden eyelids. All he wanted now was sleep.

"That was nice," Margaret whispered.

Fargo grunted.

"We can do it again tomorrow night if you're so inclined."

"If you want," Fargo mumbled.

"I haven't felt this good in ages."

Fargo seemed to recollect her husband had been dead less than a month.

"You are something."

"What I am," Fargo said, "is tired. And I can't get to sleep for all your prattle."

"Oh," Margaret said.

Fargo succumbed to slumber. He woke up twice. Once along about the middle of the night, feeling cold. He pulled his bearskin coat tighter and the blankets higher. The second time was toward dawn when a sound brought him around. He sleepily raised his head but the Ovaro showed no sign of alarm, so he went back to sleep.

When next he opened his eyes, the pitch of night had given way to the gray of impending daybreak.

Margaret was already awake and looking at him.

"You're up early," Fargo said.

"I woke up a few minutes ago," she said. "I'm just lying here admiring you."

"I'll get coffee on." Fargo needed two or three cups to start the new day.

"There's no hurry."

"If we push," Fargo said, "we can maybe reach Fort Laramie by the end of the week."

"No," Margaret said, rather sadly. "We won't."

"I tell you we can," Fargo said. He should know. He'd been there plenty of times.

"This is as far as you go," Margaret said.

Fargo was about to ask her what the hell she was talking about when a hard object was jammed against the back of his head and he heard the click of a gun hammer.

5

Fargo froze.

Margaret gazed past him and smiled. "I was worried you wouldn't find us."

"Have I ever let you down?" Fletcher said, and stepped around Fargo, holding a Spencer leveled at his head.

Fletcher wasn't alone.

Lector and Hector came up on either side, holding six-shooters.

"I bet he's plumb surprised to see us," Lector said with a grin.

"Didn't count on this, did you, mister?" Hector taunted.

"She pulls the wool over most everybody's eyes," Fletcher said, and laughed. "Don't you, darling?"

Fargo looked at Margaret. "Darling?" he growled.

"Fletch and me are like this," Margaret said, and twined the first two fingers on her left hand. "That business about Clyde? I made it up. There was no Clyde. I've never been married. Never want to be, to tell you the truth."

"You wouldn't know the truth if it bit you on the ass."

"Don't be mean just because I tricked you," Margaret said. Fussing with her hair, she stood and stepped away from him. "He's all yours, fellows."

Fletcher wagged the Spencer. "Real slow, sit up and put your arms out from your sides."

What choice did Fargo have? Fuming mad, more at himself than at them, he complied.

"Lector," Fletcher said. "Take his Colt. Do it careful. Something tells me this one is more dangerous than most."

"How dangerous can he be with us pointing three guns at him?" Lector scoffed. Nonetheless, he sidled up with his revolver cocked and pressed it to Fargo's ribs as he relieved him of the Colt. Then he scooted back, and chuckled.

Fletcher relaxed a little. Turning his head partway but not taking his eyes off Fargo, he said, "Hector, fetch the horses."

"Will do."

"Can I lower my arms?" Fargo asked, and when Fletcher nodded, he not only lowered them—he shifted around so he faced his captors. Drawing his knees to his chest, he draped his arms around his legs.

"You must feel pretty stupid along about now," Fletcher remarked.

Fargo glared at Margaret, who was kindling the fire. "Was there an old couple with their granddaughter or was that a lie too?"

"There was," Fletcher said.

Lector nodded. "They had fine china in their wagon, and jewelry and more."

"Had," Fargo said. "So they are dead, just like I thought."

"Afraid so," Margaret said.

"You killed the little girl too?"

"We couldn't hardly leave a witness, now, could we?" Fletcher said. "We did her quick, though. I saw to that. One shot through the head."

"Why am I still breathing?" Fargo wondered.

It was Margaret who answered. "Fletch likes to crow. I tell him and tell him that he should get it over with but he likes to rub it in." She broke a piece of branch and fed the pieces to the growing flames.

"We all have our failings," Fletcher said. "Mine is that I rob and kill folks."

"Is Wilbur in on it?"

"We couldn't hardly do it without him," Margaret said, and laughed.

"I'll have to settle with him, then, too," Fargo remarked.

"Mister, you won't be settling with anybody," Fletcher said. "In a few minutes you'll be dead."

Fargo's blanket was bundled about his boots. They didn't notice as he slipped his fingers into his right boot and palmed the Arkansas toothpick in its ankle sheath.

"Dead, dead, dead," Lector crowed, and cackled. "That's the part I like best."

"Any chance I can have a last request?" Fargo asked.

"Since you put it so nicely," Fletcher said.

"A cup of coffee, is all."

Fletcher shook his head in amusement. "Make him one," he commanded Margaret.

"I have to heat the pot first."

"Then do it."

"I don't like when you talk to me like that," Margaret complained.

"You're mine, aren't you? I'll talk to you any damn way I please."

Just then Hector came along the bluff leading four horses. "Here they are," he announced.

"I can see that," Fletcher said. Taking a step back, he squatted, his rifle still trained on Fargo. "Let's all have some coffee to warm us before we head back."

His hand hidden by the blanket, Fargo eased the toothpick from his boot.

"Let's see," Fletcher went on. "You'll make the tenth we've done in."

"Eleven," Margaret corrected him. "You keep forgetting that drummer."

"He wasn't worth the killing. He didn't have anything

on him but a few dollars and those damn perfumes he was selling."

"Who wants to smell like flowers?" Lector said.

"We don't rob everybody who stops," Fletcher enlightened Fargo. "Only those who have things we can sell. That old couple had a lot of stuff."

"Fine things," Margaret said.

Fargo was curious. "You never keep any of it for yourself?"

"Goodness, no," Margaret said. "Someone might come along looking for them and see it. No, most we sell to others who stop by or take it to Fort Laramie and sell it to the pilgrims bound for Oregon."

"Tell him everything, why don't you?" Fletcher said.

"Why are you being so mean to me this morning?" Margaret asked.

"As if you can't guess."

"Not that again," Margaret said. "How many times must I tell you it's you and only you."

"Did you sleep with him or not?" Fletcher asked.

"Uh-oh," Lector said.

"Not that again," Hector said.

Margaret was checking how much coffee was left in the pot.

"I asked you a question," Fletcher said.

"For your information," Margaret said without looking up, "I did not."

Fletcher looked at Fargo. "Is that true?"

"Hell, no," Fargo said. "I screwed her five times. We didn't hardly sleep all night."

"He's lying to get your goat," Margaret said. "You saw we were asleep when you snuck up on him."

"That doesn't prove anything," Fletcher said. "I wouldn't put it past you. You like it too much. You've done it with Wilbur. I know you have even though you deny it."

"Oh, hell," Lector said. "I'm so tired of hearing this."

"Me too," Hector said.

"Both of you shut up," Fletcher snapped. "This is between her and me."

"I do what I have to for the both of us," Margaret said wearily. "You know that."

Fargo was mulling how he might turn this to his advantage. His initial notion was to goad Fletcher into lowering the rifle and hitting her but now he had a different idea. "She's right," he said.

"What?" Fletcher said.

Margaret glanced around, her eyebrows puckered quizzically.

"I'm lying to make you mad," Fargo confessed. "We didn't make love. I wanted to but she said she wasn't interested."

"Margaret not interested?" Lector said.

"How's that possible?" Hector said.

Fletcher turned his glare on them. "I will by God shoot the both of you."

"We know how she is," Lector said.

"Boy, do we," Hector echoed.

Margaret was still giving Fargo a puzzled look.

"She told me that she had someone she cared for." Fargo laid it on thick. "And she wanted to be true to whoever it was."

Fletcher turned toward her and smiled, his rifle muzzle dipping toward the ground. "Well, now. I'm right pleased to hear that."

"Thank you for telling the truth," Margaret said to Fargo.

"No reason not to," Fargo said. He was worried she'd guess what he was up to; she appeared to be the brains of the bunch. To distract her he asked, "What did you do with the bodies of the old couple and the girl?"

"That's none of your business."

"What do you want to know for?" Lector asked.

"Knowing wouldn't do you any good," Hector said.

Fletcher cradled his rifle in the crook of his elbow. "How's that coffee coming?"

"It will take a few minutes, as cold as it got last night," Margaret answered.

Lector said, "I could sure use a cup."

"I'm about froze," Hector said, "from all the riding we did."

"We had to catch up," Fletcher said.

"And to think," Lector said, "Wilbur is back at the trading post, nice and warm and cozy."

"We couldn't close up and have all of us come, now, could we?" Fletcher said.

Fargo moved the blanket bundled about his boots so it wouldn't hamper him when the time came.

The sun was almost up, the eastern sky pink with splashes of orange and yellow.

Margaret noticed the colors, too. "I do so love sunrise," she said happily. "It's like the first day of creation."

"What are you talking about?" Lector said. "The sun is the sun."

"I like it too because we can see ourselves once the sun is up," Hector said.

"You're a marvel," Fletcher said.

Margaret touched the coffeepot and gave Fargo another puzzled look. "I must say," she said suspiciously, "you're taking this awful calmly."

Fargo shrugged. "I don't have a gun and the three of them do."

"Don't forget that," Lector said.

Fletcher patted his rifle. "I'll make it quick for you, too. A shot to the brain and it'll be over."

"You're all heart," Fargo said.

6

The scent of burning wood, the aroma of brewing coffee, the crunch of Lector's soles as he paced to keep warm—all of Fargo's senses were heightened. Whether he lived out the day depended on what happened in the next few minutes.

Margaret touched the pot again. "Almost ready," she announced.

"It doesn't have to be all that hot," Fletcher said.

"I like it hot," Hector said.

"What good is cold coffee?" Lector said.

"The hotter, the better," Fargo threw in. Without being obvious, he watched Fletcher's every expression, every move. It would be Fletcher first because he was closest.

Then Lector stepped in front of him and leveled the six-gun. "I plumb forgot. I'll take that poke of yours now if you don't mind and even if you do."

"It can wait until he's dead," Fletcher said.

"No, it can't," Lector replied. "I want to be sure how much is in it."

"Are you saying I'd cheat you?"

Lector looked at Fletcher. "I only want to count it so we know."

"Me too," Hector said. He, too, took his eyes off Fargo to look at Fletcher.

Switching the Arkansas toothpick from his right hand to his left, Fargo heaved up off the ground. He thrust the doubled-edged blade to the hilt into Lector's belly and ripped upward even as he grabbed the six-gun and wrested it from Lector's grasp.

"Oh!" Lector exclaimed.

Warm blood and wet gore spurted over Fargo's left hand. With his right he swept the revolver up and fired at Fletcher just as Fletcher jerked his rifle up to shoot him. Fargo's slug struck the receiver with a loud *whang* and glanced off, knocking the rifle from Fletcher's grasp.

"Damn it!" Hector cried as he was raising his own six-shooter.

Margaret screamed.

Fargo shot Hector in the head. He shifted to shoot at Fletcher again but Fletcher had darted around the horses and Fargo couldn't get a clear shot.

Lector was still on his feet. He staggered back and the toothpick slid out. Stumbling, his hands splayed over the wound, he mewed like a kitten.

Margaret flung herself at Fargo. Wrapping her arms around his legs, she hollered, "I have him, Fletch!"

Fargo clubbed her.

Fletcher was on a horse, bent low over the saddle horn and reining around to flee.

Fargo raised the revolver to shoot him but Fletcher swung over the side, Comanche fashion, and flew eastward. Fargo snapped off a shot anyway and was sure he missed. He cocked the hammer to fire again only to see the horse plunge into cottonwoods.

"Damn," Fargo said.

"I hurt," Lector bleated. The front of his clothes were a mess. He tottered and whimpered and fell to his knees in the fire. He didn't seem to realize it and knelt there as his pants began to smolder. "What's that smell?" he said.

Fargo kicked him out of the flames. He threw the revolver to the ground and snatched up his Colt and cocked it but there was no one to shoot. Hector was dead, Margaret unconscious, Fletcher gone.

Lector groaned. "I'm done for."

"You rob and kill folks," Fargo said, "odds are you die young."

"Don't lecture me," Lector said. "My pa was always lecturing me and I couldn't abide it." Closing his eyes, he groaned. "How could you do this to me?"

"There's a jackass born every minute," Fargo said.

"I'd hit you if I didn't hurt so much."

Fargo pointed his Colt. "I'll put you out of your misery."

"No!" Lector cried, his eyes going wide. "Let me go natural."

"Don't blubber then," Fargo said.

"Damn, you are hard."

Fargo squatted and wiped the toothpick clean on Hector's pants.

"Fletch was right about you. You are more dangerous than most."

"I'm still breathing," Fargo said.

"Fletcher should have shot you right off."

Fargo finished wiping and slid the toothpick into his ankle sheath.

"I didn't know you had that," Lector said.

"No one thought to look. As robbers you'd make good store clerks."

"First you kill me and now you insult me."

"Hush up and die," Fargo said.

"I will not," Lector said. "I deserve to say my piece. These are my last moments and I'm entitled."

"Nothing says I have to listen."

"You've already gutted me like a fish. What else can you do?"

"This," Fargo said, and shot him between the eyes.

For the briefest of instants, astonishment was mirrored in Lector's eyes. Then it faded along with his life as he sank to the ground and let out a last long breath.

Fargo stood and scanned the snow-covered terrain for

a sign of Fletcher. His instincts told him Fletcher would head for the trading post to warn George Wilbur. He'd head there, too, but first things, first.

It took only a minute to drag Lector and Hector a few yards from the fire. Filling his cup with steaming coffee, he sat with his back to the bluff.

By now the sun had risen and the vault of sky was a bright sea blue splashed by a few white clouds.

Fargo sipped and relished the warmth. "Damn, I was lucky," he said to himself. He was about done with his first cup when Margaret moaned and stirred and her eyes blinked open. "Rise and shine."

"You hit me."

"It could be worse," Fargo said. "You could be Lector or Hector."

Margaret groggily rose onto her elbows. She looked around, saw the bodies, and showed no more emotion than if they were squashed beetles. "Both of them?"

"Babes in the woods," Fargo said.

Stiffening in alarm, Margaret rose higher. "Fletcher?" she said. "Did you kill him too?"

"Your lover lit a shuck."

She couldn't hide her relief. "He got away?" Sinking back down, she said breathlessly, "Thank God."

"He thinks he did. It's not over."

That got her attention. "What are you fixing to do?"

"Head for the trading post."

"And I suppose you'll force me to go along?"

"Or I can shoot you."

Margaret's eyes bored into him like twin drills. "You would, wouldn't you? You have no qualms at all about it. What manner of man are you?"

"Says the bitch who had hand in killing a ten-year-old girl."

"Fletch did her, not me."

"All the same," Fargo said.

35

Margaret sat up and brushed at her dress. "I imagine you'll want me to help you bury them."

"Who?"

"Lector and Hector, of course. Surely you're not going to leave them lying there like that."

"Surely I am." Fargo refilled his cup. One more and they would be on their way.

"That's mean," Margaret said. "Everyone deserves a proper burial."

"Bastards don't." Fargo smiled. "Bitches neither."

Anger got the better of her. "Quit calling me that. I won't be talked to that way. Not by someone I've shared my body with."

"Out of true love," Fargo said.

"Go to hell."

"You bedded me so I'd sleep more soundly and make it easier for Fletcher and the simpletons."

"I bedded you because you're handsome," Margaret said. "That, and I like to fuck."

"Finally some honesty." Fargo gestured with his cup. "Have some if you want. We're in for another cold day."

Margaret had been eyeing the pot. She eagerly filled a cup and held it in both hands and sipped. Coincidentally, or so she wanted it to appear, she shifted so she was a little nearer to him.

"You should keep in mind what you said," Fargo warned.

"Which was?"

"I have no qualms about shooting you if you try to throw that coffee in my face and grab my gun."

"I wasn't thinking any such thing," Margaret said, but it was plain by her face and her tone that she was. She fell into a sulk and it was a couple of minutes before she ventured, "I have a proposition for you."

"I don't want a second helping," Fargo said. "One was enough."

"Not *that*, you bastard. I wouldn't let you touch me again for all the gold in creation."

"Yes, you would."

Margaret shrugged. "Maybe. But my proposition has to do with money. I have over five hundred dollars in a hidey-hole at the trading post. It's yours if you'll let me have a horse and go."

Fargo shook his head.

"Why the hell not?"

"That old couple and their granddaughter."

"Them again. What are they to you? You didn't even know them."

"You killed a little girl."

Margaret scowled. "So that's it. You have a soft spot."

"There are some things a person doesn't do. That's one of them."

"I keep telling you it was Fletcher who pulled the trigger. I've never killed anyone."

"So you say."

"I find out stuff, is all. People will open up to a female where they won't to a man."

"And you found out about the old couple's china and their other valuables," Fargo guessed. "Their blood is on your hands the same as the others."

"Fine," Margaret spat. "Be this way."

"Did you know that you drool when your dander is up?"

Without thinking, Margaret touched her mouth. "Bastard. Do you know what? I can't wait for you to try and take Fletcher. He's not Lector or Hector. He's clever and he's quick, and it'll be you the buzzards feed on, not him."

"We'll find out soon enough," Fargo said.

7

From a distance the trading post appeared peaceful. No horses were at the hitch rail. No wagons were parked out front.

The only sign of life was the smoke that curled from the stone chimney.

Fargo sat his saddle with the Henry in his hand. Behind the Ovaro stood the string of horses that belonged to the outlaws.

On one of them, glaring her spite, was Margaret. Her hands were tied behind her back, her feet were lashed to her stirrups. He'd also stuffed a gag in her mouth.

"I reckon I'll have a look-see." Fargo grinned at her. "Sit tight until I get back."

Margaret muttered something through the gag. He couldn't understand the words but her meaning was plain.

Fargo pricked his spurs to the stallion and advanced at a cautious walk.

There was no sign of Fletcher's horse but it could be hidden nearby.

Fargo kept expecting either Fletcher or Wilbur to appear at the front door or the window and blaze away but no one did.

A glance down the trail to the southeast showed it was empty for as far as the eye could see.

Good, Fargo reflected. He didn't need busybodies butting in.

Ten yards out Fargo drew rein. Sliding off, he crouched and ran to the near corner. Sidling to the window, he risked a quick peek. What he saw made no sense.

George Wilbur was over at the bar, doing what he seemed to always be doing: cleaning glasses. He was whistling to himself.

A trick, Fargo figured. He moved to the front door. As quietly as he could, he worked the latch, and when it was free, he kicked the door and exploded inside.

Wilbur froze with a glass in one hand and a towel in the other. "What in the world!" he exclaimed.

Fargo centered the Henry on the man's chest. "Where's Fletcher?"

"How would I know?" Wilbur replied.

"Don't pretend," Fargo growled. "He came back to warn you."

"Warn me about what?" Wilbur asked. He seemed genuinely confused.

Fargo glanced at the hall to the back but no one came charging out.

Wilbur set down the glass. "Listen, mister, what is this?"

"I know everything," Fargo said. "I know about the old couple and their granddaughter. I know they weren't the first you've killed and robbed."

"I haven't killed anyone," Wilbur said indignantly.

"Bullshit."

"I'm telling you the truth."

Fargo strode to the bar. The Henry's muzzle was barely a foot from Wilbur's swarthy face. "I should splatter your brains."

"I wouldn't harm a soul."

"You were part of it. This is your trading post. You let them pick and do the killing but you take a share."

"Whoever told you that was lying," Wilbur said. He was pasty with fear, and nervously licked his lips.

"I'll ask you one last time. Where the hell is Fletcher?"

"I haven't seen him since he and the other two rode out of here after you and Margaret," Wilbur said. "Honest."

Damned if Fargo didn't believe him. That meant Fletcher hadn't come back to warn Wilbur but had cut out for parts unknown. Saving his own hide, apparently, was more important to Fletcher than anything else.

"Where's your share of the loot?"

"The what?"

Fargo touched the muzzle to Wilbur's forehead. "Keep treating me like I'm a jackass and see what happens."

"I don't know what you're talking about. Honest to God, I don't."

"I'm handing you over to the army," Fargo informed him. "And with any luck, you'll be hung."

"You're not a lawman. I refuse to go anywhere with you."

"Fine. I'd just as soon shoot you anyway."

Wilbur stared into Fargo's eyes, and whatever he saw made him swallow. "How about if we strike a deal?"

"Ah," Fargo said. "I thought you were innocent?"

"You agree to let me go, and I show you."

"Show me what?"

"You have to see for yourself."

Fargo took a step back. "There's nothing you could show me that would change my mind."

"Yes, there is. Trust me."

Fargo snorted.

"We have to go in the back. To the kitchen."

"Why there?"

"You have to see with your own eyes."

"Fine," Fargo said. "Lead the way. But one wrong twitch and you're dead."

"I believe you."

Wilbur slowly walked to the end of the bar and over to the hall. He jumped when Fargo jammed the Henry against his spine but he didn't try anything as he led the way to the kitchen and across to a square door in the floor.

"The root cellar?" Fargo said. "What in hell's down there."

"Open it and find out."

"No," Fargo said. He didn't know what game the man was playing at but he would see it through. "Open it yourself."

Wilbur bent, gripped the rope handle and lifted. The door swung up easily. "There," he said with a nod. "They didn't want anyone to know."

It was a little girl, tied hand and foot and with a bandanna over her mouth. She was on her side amid a slab of deer meat, a pile of potatoes, a basket of carrots, and more.

She looked up in stark terror, her face streaked with dry tears.

"It's the granddaughter," George Wilbur said. "Jessie Cavanaugh."

Fargo glared and raised the Henry.

"Wait!" Wilbur cried, throwing his hands up. "It wasn't me who tied her. It was Fletcher. He figured to give her as a gift. His very words."

"A gift?" Fargo said.

"To Blackjack Tar. Ever heard of him?"

Of course Fargo had. Tar was the scourge of the territory; for five or six years he'd been robbing and killing to his vile heart's content. The things he did to his victims made Apaches seem tame.

Wilbur had gone on. "Fletcher and Blackjack Tar are friends. They used to ride together."

"Son of a bitch," Fargo said, and lowered the Henry a few inches.

Wilbur exhaled. "You're not going to kill me, then?"

"No," Fargo said, and clubbed him with the stock. He didn't hold back. The blow slammed Wilbur off his feet and he fell flat and didn't move.

Fargo hiked his boot to stomp the man's face but set his leg down again.

Jessie Cavanaugh was watching.

"I won't hurt you, girl," Fargo said, starting down the short flight of steps. "I heard about your grandpa and grandma, and I'm sorry."

Tears welled, and the child bowed her head and uttered a choking sob.

Fargo wanted to kick himself. He leaned the rifle against the steps, drew his toothpick, and made short shrift of the ropes. He expected her to cower in fright, and to have to coax her out. To his surprise, no sooner did he undo the bandanna than she wrapped her arms around him and pressed her face to his chest.

"Thank you, thank you, thank you," she sobbed.

A knot formed in Fargo's throat. Coughing to clear it, he told her his name. "We have to get out of here. One of the gang is still on the loose."

She looked up with such gratitude and warmth, it made him uncomfortable. "You saved me."

"Anyone would," was all Fargo could think of to say.

"What happened to the bad woman? Is she dead? She treated me awful. She hit me and teased me."

"Did she, now?" Fargo said. "No, she's still alive. We'll turn her over to the law."

"She stabbed my grandma. I'd like to stab her."

"We have to go." Fargo stood and helped her stand. He grabbed the Henry and saw her stumble. He hooked an arm around her to keep her from falling.

"Sorry," Jessie said. "My legs won't work."

"How long have they had you tied down here?"

"I don't know how many days but it's been an awful long while."

"I'll carry you," Fargo said, and did, up the steps and

across the kitchen and down the hall to the bar. He set her on the end, steadied her, and said, "I'll be right back." He turned, but she clutched his arm.

"Don't leave me alone. Please."

"I have to get the man in the kitchen."

"I'll go with you."

"I'll only be a minute. I'll drag him out here and tie him and then we'll be on our way."

"I'd sure like a bite to eat first," Jessie said. "I'm so hungry."

"I suppose I can fix you something. But we can't take too long."

"I understand," Jessie said. "You're worried about the other man." She paused. "Which one is it, anyhow?"

"Fletcher."

At the mention, new terror twisted her face. "Him!" she exclaimed. "He used to come down and sit and tell me all the things that Blackjack Tar was going to do to me." She shuddered.

"He doesn't know it yet but he doesn't have very long to live," Fargo assured her. "As soon as you're safe, I aim to track him down."

"Better be careful," Jessie said. "Once he bragged that he's killed seventeen people. Do you think that's true?"

"Let's forget about him for now." Fargo went to go but she held on.

"I'm scared."

"I know." Fargo patted her shoulder. "It will only take me a minute. I'll be right back."

"Promise?"

Fargo nodded.

Reluctantly, Jessie let go. Only then did he notice that her wrists had been scraped raw by the rope and realized the pain she must be in.

A sadness came over her, a sorrow beyond her tender years. "I didn't know people could be so terrible," she said softly.

"Stay put," Fargo said. He smiled and hurried down the hall. He was thinking of what she had gone through and not about what he was doing, and he'd taken several steps into the kitchen before he saw that George Wilbur wasn't lying by the root cellar. "What the hell?" he blurted.

That was when Wilbur charged from behind the stove waving a meat cleaver.

8

Fargo barely had time to raise the Henry to ward off the blow. Wilbur was stronger than he looked. Fargo was knocked back a step and nearly lost his hold on the rifle. He swung the stock at Wilbur's head but Wilbur ducked and slashed the cleaver at his chest. Skipping aside, Fargo slipped. He tried to regain his balance, and couldn't. He came down hard on his back and went to level the Henry but Wilbur was already on him.

The meat cleaver sheared at Fargo's face. Again he got the Henry up. Metal rang on metal.

Wilbur was red with rage. His mouth was working but all that came out were bestial growls. He kicked at the Henry and it went flying.

Fargo rolled and heard the *thunk* of the cleaver as it bit into the floor. He rolled several more times as fast as he could and pushed to his feet.

With a fierce bellow, George Wilbur attacked. Fargo threw himself to one side to keep from being split like a side of meat. He clawed for his Colt—and spotted it lying where he had fallen.

Wilbur found his voice. "I've got you!" he roared. "I've got you, you bastard!"

Fargo retreated. He cast about for something to use as a weapon but all he spotted was a broom by the sink. He grabbed it anyway.

Wilbur rushed him, the cleaver gleaming in the lamp-light. Fargo raised the broom, only to have it shatter under the impact. He threw the pieces at Wilbur and retreated.

Wilbur came after him. The man was beside himself; his eyes were pits of hellfire, his face contorted; spittle dribbled from a corner of his mouth.

The cleaver clipped Fargo's hat, nicked his shoulder. He dodged, and realized they were next to the root cellar.

Wilbur's back was to the opening in the floor. He raised the meat cleaver.

Springing into the air, Fargo kicked him in the chest.

Wilbur tottered on his heels. Squawking, he frantically pinwheeled his arms but it did no good. He squawked again as he went over the edge.

Whirling, Fargo ran to the Colt. He sank to a knee and scooped it up as Wilbur hurtled up out of the cellar. "Drop it!" he warned, but Wilbur was too far gone to heed.

Wilbur charged.

Fargo fanned the Colt once, twice, three times. By then Wilbur was only a few feet away, and buckling. His body slid to a stop barely a foot from Fargo's leg, the meat cleaver brushing his boot.

"Damn," Fargo said. He rolled Wilbur over and felt for a pulse to be sure.

"Is he dead, mister?" Jessie Cavanaugh asked.

Fargo turned. She was in the doorway, looking remarkably calm for a little girl who had just seen a man gunned down. "He's dead."

"Good," Jessie said. "He was a bad man like those others."

"I told you to stay up front."

"I couldn't," she said. "I was too afraid." She looked hopefully about the kitchen. "Can I have some food now? My tummy hurts, it's so empty."

Fargo considered dragging the body out and decided not to. She didn't seem disturbed by it, and she was starved. "Have a seat," he said, with a nod at a chair by the table.

Instead Jessie came over and stared at George Wilbur. "Do you know what he said to me?"

Fargo shook his head while reloading.

"He said he wished I was older. Why did he say a thing like that?"

Fargo wasn't about to tell her.

"He wasn't as mean as that lady or the other man but he wasn't nice, either. Not after Grandpa and Grandma—" Jessie stopped.

"Have a seat, I said."

Jessie fixed her moist eyes on him. "Why did it happen, mister? Why did God let them die with my grandpa begging and my grandma screaming like she did?"

"Hell, girl," Fargo said. "Ask God."

"I did," Jessie said. "When I was in the root cellar. I prayed like Grandma taught me and I asked why they had to die."

"And?" Fargo prompted when she didn't go on.

"I never got an answer."

Fargo twirled the Colt into his holster. He gently moved Jessie to the chair, and she sat without complaint. He was going to cook some venison but when he opened a cupboard he found a bowl with a dozen eggs. "I reckon I'll join you," he said.

Once the stove was hot enough, he scrambled the whole dozen. He also buttered slices of toast and brewed coffee.

Jessie watched everything he did. She didn't take her eyes off him once, as if she were afraid he might disappear.

"Do you hear that?" she asked as he brought their plates over.

Her stomach was rumbling.

"Dig in," Fargo said. He was famished, too, and wolfed

his food before she was halfway finished. "I have to go check on something," he said. Or, specifically, someone— he'd left Margaret alone too long.

"No!" Jessie cried, gripping his hand. "Wait! Please. I'm almost done."

Against his better judgment, Fargo gave in. When she forked the last morsel of egg into her mouth, he grabbed her hand and hastened to the front door.

The Ovaro and the other horses were where he had left them.

Margaret and her horse weren't.

Fargo rose onto his toes but he didn't see her.

"Where's the bad lady?" Jessie asked.

"Let's find out." Only then did something occur to him. "Do you have a coat? And can you ride?"

"I think the woman had my clothes in her closet. And yes, I can ride a little. Grandma was teaching me."

"You'll have to ride double with me then."

"I'd like that."

They found her bag in Margaret's room. Jessie shrugged into a heavy coat, and they took the bag with them.

Fargo swung her onto the Ovaro, carefully climbed on so as not to bump her with his leg, and rode in a circle. He found what he was looking for.

Fresh prints pointed to the northwest.

Gripping the lead rope to the other horses, Fargo gigged the Ovaro.

While he'd been inside the sky had gone from blue to mostly gray. Swift-moving clouds scudded. The temperature had dropped, too.

"Do you think it's going to snow?" Jessie asked.

"Most likely," Fargo answered. The weather in that neck of the country was fickle; wait five minutes and it nearly always changed. Sometimes fronts that seemed to portend rain or snow didn't let loose a drop. Other times, torrents and blizzards swept out of nowhere.

"I like snow," Jessie said. "We haven't seen much of it but Grandma said we would before too long."

Fargo wanted to tell her not to talk but couldn't after all she'd been through. He figured if he didn't respond she'd go quiet. Not so.

"I loved her so much. Grandpa too. They took me in after my ma died. She got consumption, the doctor called it. She was all skinny and coughed a lot. I prayed for her to get better but she didn't."

Fargo's jaw muscles twitched.

"Pa was killed when I was eight. He got run over by a wagon and his neck was broke. Did you ever hear of such a thing? I cried and cried. He used to tuck me in at night and have me say my prayers. Did your pa and ma tuck you in?"

"I was older than you when I lost my folks." Fargo didn't go into detail.

"It's awful people have to die. Why can't we be born and live forever? That makes more sense."

Fargo imagined all the willing fillies he could bed if he lived that long, and grinned.

"What's that up ahead?"

Fargo looked. He'd been concentrating on the tracks. "I'll be damned," he said.

"You shouldn't cuss. Ma and Grandma said it's not nice to cuss."

"It's all right for me to do," Fargo said.

"How come?"

"I'm a scout and cussing is what scouts do."

"I didn't know."

Margaret hadn't gotten far. Apparently her cinch had loosened and her saddle had shifted, and there she was, hanging nearly upside down, her feet still tied fast to the stirrups, her hands still bound behind her back. She was furiously working to free herself.

She heard them coming, and glanced up. "Hell," she said.

"The mean lady cusses a lot too," Jessie remarked.

Fargo drew rein, leaned on his saddle horn, and grinned.

"Well?" Margaret said. "Are you going to leave me hanging like this?"

"I'm thinking about it," Fargo said.

"Bastard."

"Hello, mean lady," Jessie said. "Remember me?"

"You little snot," Margaret said. "We should have killed you when we killed your grandparents, the doting old fools."

"Did you hear her?" Jessie asked. "Why does she talk like that?"

"She's a bitch," Fargo said.

Margaret uttered a string of invective a river rat would envy.

"Oh my," Jessie said. "She should be a scout like you."

Dismounting, Fargo stepped up to Margaret, bent, and slugged her in the gut. Not with all his strength but hard enough that she cried out and writhed in pain.

"You miserable, rotten son of a bitch," she spat when she subsided.

Hunkering, Fargo seized her by the hair and turned her face to his. "Here's how it will be. From now on, keep your mouth shut unless I say you can talk."

Margaret opened her mouth to say something but he cocked his fist and she closed it again.

"When you talk to the girl, talk nice. Nothing about her grandma or grandpa. Try to escape and I'll shoot you in the leg. Try to run the horses off and I'll shoot you in both legs. Try to hurt Jessie and you join Lector and Hector and George Wilbur in whatever hereafter there is."

"God, I hate you."

Fargo slugged her a second time.

Margaret thrashed so violently, it was a wonder she didn't tear the saddle loose.

Jessie giggled and said, "That isn't very nice."

To redo the cinch, Fargo first had to untie both of Margaret's legs and dump her on the ground. When he finished and reached for her, she shook his hand off and stood on her own. Moving stiffly, she climbed on.

As Fargo turned to the Ovaro, white flakes began to fall.

"Oh look!" Jessie cried in delight. "Snow!"

9

By the time they had gone a mile there were two inches on the ground. By later afternoon, five inches.

"Isn't it pretty?" Jessie said.

Fargo supposed it was the continual parade of large fluffy flakes falling so gently to earth. He was too concerned with where they'd make camp and how deep the snow would get to admire it.

Visibility was a few dozen yards, if that. Without the sun to guide him, he had to rely on his sense of direction. Fortunately, it seldom failed him. He stuck to a northwesterly course, as near as he could.

A belt of woods offered haven.

Fargo found a small clearing where the trees sheltered them from the worst of the snow and the wind. He set about stripping their animals and getting a fire going. He left Margaret trussed on her side and took Jessie with him when he gathered firewood. She cheerfully helped. He'd forgotten that children bounced back from tragedy a lot quicker than adults. Or maybe they were just better at hiding their feelings.

With a fire crackling and coffee on, his spirits improved. He'd brought food from the trading post, including flour, and cooked biscuits for the girl to go with the pemmican stew he made. It wasn't exactly a feast but it tasted right fine.

"What about me?" Margaret asked. He had removed

her gag when he dumped her on the ground. Not because he wanted to. Jessie asked him to do it.

Fargo dipped his biscuit into the gravy, took a bite, and smacked his lips. "What about you?"

"Don't I get to eat?"

"No."

Jessie looked up from her tin plate. "That wouldn't be right."

"An empty belly will do her wonders," Fargo said.

"My grandma said we always have to be nice to people, even when they're not nice to us."

"Your grandma is dead," Fargo said, and regretted it the moment the words were out of his mouth. "If you want, give her a little of your food." He'd be damned if he would.

Jessie hunkered and spooned the stew slowly so as not to spill it.

"Thank you, little one," Margaret said after her first swallow. "You know, it wasn't my doing. Your grandparents, I mean. It was Fletcher's idea, him and the others."

Fargo was around the fire in two long strides. Sinking to a knee, he grabbed Margaret by the throat, and squeezed. She struggled, but there was nothing she could do. When her face was near purple and she was gasping for breath, he said, "Try that again and you won't like what happens." He let go.

Margaret doubled over, coughing and wheezing.

Jessie was agog. "What did she do?"

"She's trying to cozy up to you, pretending she's your friend."

"Oh. Don't worry. I know she's not. I'd never trust her."

Fargo grunted. He went back around and sat crosslegged. The snow had tapered but not stopped entirely. It was full dark and soon the temperature would take a drastic drop.

Margaret's face was a mask of murderous hate. She coughed and shook and finally lay still.

53

"I know it was you killed my grandma," Jessie said to her. "How could you do that?"

Margaret didn't reply.

"I don't think I'll feed you any more," Jessie said. "Mr. Fargo is right. You don't deserve any food."

"Go to hell."

Fargo figured the girl was so worn out she'd turn in early but she came and sank down next to him and talked his ears off about the pet dog she'd had once, about her pet cat, about her friends, about how she liked to help her ma in the kitchen, and how her pa had a beard just like his. He didn't have to say much; he'd nod and she took that as a sign he was interested.

Fargo felt sorry for her. Without parents and grandparents, she'd be put up for adoption. And there weren't a lot of people beating down the door to adopt these days, or so he'd heard. Something to do with most folks thought adopted kids were more bother than they were worth. Sounded cruel to him, but there it was.

It took a while, but Jessie talked herself out.

He spread blankets and saw to it she was bundled close enough to the fire to keep warm and started to turn away.

"Wait. Don't you want to hear me say my prayers? Ma and Grandma always did."

"Say them to yourself," Fargo said, marveling that she could.

"All right." Jessie clasped her hands and her mouth moved silently.

Fargo saw Margaret smirk and he almost hit her. When Jessie was done he pulled the blanket higher and sat across from her where he could keep an eye on them both, the Henry in his lap.

He wasn't worried about hostiles. Few would be abroad in the bad weather, and fewer still this close to the fort. Wild beasts were another matter. And Fletcher was out there, somewhere.

He stayed awake as long as he could. Along about two his eyelids grew so heavy that he curled on his side and let himself drift off. Margaret was snoring so he reckoned it was safe.

The fire, the quiet, he slept like one dead until shortly before the break of day.

Awaking with a start, he sat bolt upright. The air had a smoky scent.

Jessie and Margaret were still asleep.

Relieved, Fargo kindled the fire. He made oatmeal for Jessie. For him it was coffee as usual.

The snow had stopped, leaving a good eight inches. He could see his breath and that of the horses.

Margaret hadn't stirred. She lay with her arms behind her and her legs bent as he came around and sank to a knee to rouse her.

Without warning she was in motion. Her left hand shot to his Colt even as her right clawed at his eyes. Instinctively, he jerked back. He saved his eyes but her nails raked his cheek, drawing blood and hurting like hell. He grabbed her left wrist as she yanked his Colt clear and tried to grab her right wrist but missed.

Hissing like a rattler, Margaret drove her foot at his middle. He twisted but it wasn't enough. She caught him good; it felt as if his stomach tried to burst out his spine.

Fargo's vision swam. His grip on her wrist slackened. She wrenched but he held on. Suddenly he could see again, see her other hand streak to the Colt and level it at him. He struck her arm as the revolver went off, heard Jessie cry out.

Rage gripped him. Fargo punched Margaret's jaw once, twice, each blow rocking her head but she still tried to steady the Colt to shoot him. He punched her a third time, not holding back. There was a sharp *crack* and Margaret sagged.

Fargo tore the Colt from her fingers and raised it to

strike her over the head, but didn't. She was out cold. He turned, fearing what he'd see, and almost laughed in relief.

Jessie hadn't been hit by the slug. She had her hand to her throat and was wide-eyed with shock. "You hurt her!"

"She was trying to hurt me."

"Is she dead?"

"I wish."

"You don't mean that." Jessie knelt and touched Margaret's jaw where a bruise was darkening. "You hit her really hard."

"It's too bad I didn't break it."

"She'll be awful mad."

Fargo examined the ropes that had bound her. The wily bitch had burned through them, probably right before he woke up. That was the scent he'd noticed. He should have realized it sooner.

"She might try to kill you again," Jessie mentioned.

Not if Fargo could help it. He got a rope and cut new pieces and tied her wrists and ankles and added loops around her thighs for good measure. He gagged her, too.

"How will she ride like that?" Jessie wondered.

"You ask a lot of questions."

"My grandma used to say I do that because I'm only ten. Didn't you ask questions when you were my age?"

"I don't remember."

"How can anyone forget being ten?"

"There are times when I drink so much, I can't remember what I did the night before," Fargo said. Fortunately, they were few and far between.

"You drink liquor?"

"I don't drink tea."

"Grandma said that liquor is bad for you. She'd catch Grandpa taking a drink now and then and scold him worse than she scolded me when I snuck sugar."

"Some women don't let a man have any fun."

"That's not true. My grandma let Grandpa have all the fun he wanted. He could play checkers and horseshoes and sometimes he'd play hide and seek with me."

"She let him do all that?" Fargo asked as he lifted Margaret and carried her to the sorrel.

"Grandma used to say you have to give a man some play in his leash."

Fargo snorted.

"What?"

"Your grandma was some lady."

"The best in the world," Jessie said softly, and her features clouded.

Fargo tossed Margaret on belly-down. He'd saved a last length of rope and slid it under and tied her hands to her ankles.

"Won't that be uncomfortable?" Jessie asked.

Fargo smiled. "Uncomfortable as hell." Between that and her jaw she'd be miserable.

Presently they were under way.

Jessie looped her arms around his waist and rested her cheek on his back. "What will happen to me when we get to the fort?"

"I'll turn you over to Colonel Harrington. His wife is there. She'll likely look after you."

"Will they let me live with them?"

Fargo hadn't thought of that. The Harringtons had never had kids of their own and were in their early fifties. "I can't rightly say."

"What will you do?"

"Go after Fletcher."

"Because of what he did to my grandparents?"

"And what he tried to do to me."

Jessie looked up. "You're not the forgiving sort, as Grandma used to say."

"I'm sure as hell not," Fargo said.

10

Fort Laramie got its start as a trading post. When the army felt the need to establish a military presence as a bastion against hostiles and to watch over those traveling the Oregon Trail, the government bought the trading post. Some of the buildings were replaced, new ones added, and fortifications erected.

Located on the west bank of the Laramie River not far from its junction with the North Platte, the fort was an important stopping-off point for those headed west.

Fargo had been there more in the spring and summer than in the winter. It was unusual for him to see it mantled in snow, looking stark and bleak in the gloom of an overcast sky.

The snow had stopped falling but it could start again at any time.

A score of wagons was in a giant circle and half a dozen fires had been lit.

People bundled against the cold were coming and going.

The gates were open. Sentries on the ramparts kept an eye on the countryside.

Glances were cast at Fargo and Jessie. Gasps and whispers broke out at the sight of Margaret trussed up like a hog for slaughter.

A soldier on the rampart above the gate bellowed for the officer of the guard.

Fargo was relieved that it was Colonel Harrington who came. He'd known Harrington for several years, and liked him. It helped that the colonel was one of the few truly competent officers he'd come across.

Too many were too young and too green. They graduated from West Point strutting like peacocks and thinking they could wipe out every hostile west of the Mississippi River without breaking a sweat. A lot of early graves testified to their stupidity.

Harrington smiled and offered his hand. He lit up like a candle when Fargo introduced Jessie. "How do you do? I never imagined I would see my friend, here, in the company of so young a lady as yourself. Usually they are much older."

"Cute," Fargo said.

"Him or me?" Jessie asked.

Fargo stepped to the sorrel and slapped Margaret on the fanny. She raised her head and glared and cursed through her gag. "And this," he said, "is the bitch who had a hand in killing Jessie's grandparents and a lot of other folks."

Harrington listened with rising anger to the rest, and when Fargo was done, he smiled coldly at Margaret.

"Well, now. I don't believe our guardhouse has ever housed a woman but there's a first time for everything. You'll be held while we contact the proper authorities. As a civilian, your fate is in their hands. But I must say, I sincerely hope they hang you."

Margaret did more swearing.

The colonel issued commands and a pair of husky troopers bore her off. "As for you, young lady," he said to Jessie, "I'll have Sergeant Petrie take you to my wife. Ethel will be delighted to make your acquaintance."

Jessie gripped Fargo's hand and moved behind his leg so only her head peeked out. "I'd rather stay with Skye."

"We have a lot to talk about, him and I," Harrington said. "You'll like my wife. Believe me."

Jessie looked up. "What do I do?"

Squatting, Fargo grinned and touched her chin. "We've talked about this. Ethel is as nice as your grandma. She'll look after you."

"I want you to look after me."

"I have work to do. I can't be with you every minute."

"You'll come see me as soon as you're done with your talk? You promise?"

Fargo nodded.

Reluctantly, Jessie let the sergeant lead her off by the hand. She looked back the whole way, not taking her eyes off Fargo until they had gone around the headquarters.

"She seems quite fond of you," Colonel Harrington remarked.

"Don't even think it," Fargo said. "I'd need a wife and that's not going to happen."

"I suppose we should get to it then."

It was the middle of the afternoon and the post was at its busiest. The sutler was doing booming business with the emigrants from the wagon train. The blacksmith was repairing a broken wheel rim, the peal of his hammer clear in the icy air.

Fargo was grateful for the warmth of Harrington's office and doubly so for the coffee the colonel had his orderly bring.

Harrington began things off. "You got here sooner than I expected. Which is good."

"Your message said it was urgent," Fargo reminded him.

"And it is." Harrington rose from his chair, moved to the window, and stood staring to the west with his arms behind him, at parade rest. "This winter looks to be a bad one."

Fargo grunted.

"The snow and the cold have come early. That wagon train out front is the last due in until spring, and if they stick to the Oregon Trail, they should make it through."

Fargo swallowed and thought about asking for cream.

"There was another train that came through about three weeks ago," Harrington continued. "Their wagon master was a man by the name of Jacob Coarse. Ever hear of him?"

Fargo shook his head, then realized Harrington wasn't looking at him. "Can't say as I have, no."

"The man irritated me. He thinks he's the cock of the walk. He knows everything and won't listen to anyone who thinks differently."

"One of those."

"He believed he could get to Oregon sooner by taking a shortcut."

About to sip, Fargo paused. "I don't know of any short-cut."

"Neither do I." Harrington turned, and his face was grim. "His great idea was to cut up through the geyser country and then head due west."

"The damned fool." Fargo was as familiar as any man alive with that region. It was some of the most rugged on the continent.

"That was my opinion," Colonel Harrington said. "Of course, I had to be tactful about expressing it. I explained that wagons can't possibly make it across the Tetons but he refused to listen. He said, and I'll quote him, that he'd yet to meet the mountains he couldn't lick."

"Hell," Fargo said.

"I explained that the snows come earlier up there than they do here. That he might find him and all his charges stranded in the high country in the dead of winter with slim prospects of survival. Can you guess what his response was?"

"He's never met the winter he couldn't lick?"

Harrington smiled. "He told me that no one ever gets anywhere in life by being timid. That he was confident he could beat the snow, make it over, and have his wagon train in Oregon a week and a half sooner than he would if he took the Oregon Trail."

"Jackass."

"I tried my best to talk him out of it but it was no use. Twenty wagons were in his train. Over fifty people, counting the children. There was even a baby, as I recall."

"Yet this Coarse went anyway," Fargo said in disgust.

"Did I mention how arrogant he was? And now I hear it has cost him."

Fargo saw where this was going. "Don't tell me," he said.

"Remember Jules Vallee, the old trapper?" Harrington asked.

Fargo knew Jules well, and said so.

"He came all the way down from the Tetons to let me know that Coarse and his people are stranded. The first blizzard of the season about buried them. Jules said they're running low on food and can use our help."

"That's why you sent for me."

"You're the best scout we have," Harrington said. "And you and that horse of yours can cover more ground in a couple of days than my men can in a week."

"You want me to go up and bring them out?"

"I do. Whether Coarse wants to come or not. Do whatever is necessary. You can even use force if you have to."

"I like that part."

"You won't like the next part, I'm afraid." Harrington returned to his desk and sat with his hands folded. "Jules told me he found sign that Blackjack Tar and his bunch were keeping an eye on the train."

"Hell," Fargo said again.

"My guess is that Tar will wait until Coarse and his people are so weak from lack of food that they can't defend themselves, then move in and help himself to their money and valuables."

"And wipe them out to keep them from talking." Fargo

drained the coffee and set the cup on the desk. "This gets better and better."

"Doesn't it?" Harrington frowned. "I'm sorry. My first impulse was to take out a patrol. But I don't know the country like you do and we might not be able to find them or wind up stranded ourselves."

"Why couldn't Jules guide you?"

"I asked him to and he refused."

"He give a reason?"

"Jules wants nothing to do with Blackjack Tar. He says that Tar is poison. Since he's a civilian I couldn't force him."

"Where is Jules now?"

Colonel Harrington's frown deepened. "He fell into a bottle and has been there ever since. Has a corner to himself over in the stable. So long as he behaves I won't throw him off the post although by rights I should."

"I'll talk to him."

"Maybe he'll lead you where he wouldn't lead us," Harrington said. "But between you and me, I doubt it. He's scared to death of Tar."

"Most folks are."

"If he agrees, I'll have Captain Davies and twenty men accompany you."

"No," Fargo said. "You were right the first time. I can get there a lot faster alone and bring them down that much sooner."

"There's Tar and his killers to consider."

"They'd likely bushwhack your men." Fargo shook his head. "Why risk their lives if you don't have to?"

"I should send a few men, at least. Frankly, I don't like the thought of you tangling with the worst cutthroats in the territory all by yourself."

"Makes two of us," Fargo said.

11

A corporal was sweeping out, and when Fargo asked if Jules Vallee was there, the corporal scowled and pointed at a corner under the hayloft. "That good-for-nothing? He doesn't hardly stir except to stagger out and buy a new bottle." He resumed his sweeping. "Why the colonel doesn't get rid of him, I'll never know."

The stink was atrocious. Even the horses in their stalls turned their heads away.

At first all Fargo saw was a pile of straw. Then he noticed a foot sticking out. The moccasin had a hole in the sole and was thin from long use. He nudged it.

From under the straw came a muffled oath.

Fargo kicked the foot.

The straw shifted. "Do that again, whoever you are," a voice croaked, "and I'll whip you within an inch of your life."

Fargo chuckled. "Bold talk for someone who can't stand up straight, from what I hear."

The straw did more shifting and a head poked out. A thatch of gray hair stuck down from under a beaver hat and gray stubble sprinkled a pointed chin. Filmy gray eyes struggled to focus and finally thin lips parted in a smile. "Skye Fargo, as I live and breathe."

"Been a while, Jules."

The old trapper pushed the straw away and slowly rose. His buckskins had seen as much wear as his moccasins. Blinking and scratching, he swayed slightly as he said, "You're a welcome sight for this old coon, I can tell you that."

Fargo held out his hand. Jules shook, his palm clammy and cold. "Colonel Harrington says you're trying to drink yourself to death."

"What does he know?" Jules said irritably, and scratched under an arm.

"Harrington is a good man."

"I didn't mean nothing. It's decent of him to let me stay until the weather warms."

"You're planning to stick around until spring?" Fargo asked in mild surprise.

Nodding, Jules bent and rummaged about in the straw. He found what he was searching for, said "Ah!" and straightened with a bottle in his hand. It was empty. He shook it and upended it, and swore.

"What's gotten into you?"

"Nothing," Jules said, casting the bottle aside.

"I never knew you to drink this much."

Jules smacked his lips and gazed out of the stable. "They don't call it firewater for nothing. It keeps me warm on cold nights."

"There's more to it," Fargo guessed.

Jules shuffled past. "I need more bug juice. You're welcome to tag along if you stop blathering." He squinted at Fargo as Fargo fell into step beside him. "What are you doing here, hoss?"

"Harrington sent for me."

"Let me guess. Those peckerwoods up in the geyser country?"

"The very same," Fargo confirmed.

"Were I you, I'd decline. It won't be easy. Anything but."

"I've heard about Tar."

"He's only part of it but he's enough." Jules came to

where the pale light of the overcast sky intruded into the stable, and stopped. His eyes began to water and he shut them and grimaced as if in pain.

"I know Tar's reputation," Fargo said. "He's a bad one."

"Worse than bad. I've been around a lot longer than you and run into a lot more badmen, and he makes the rest seem like church deacons."

"He kills people but so do I when I have to."

Jules peered at him through those runny eyes. "He does it for the fun of it. For the thrill. Men, females, sprouts, it makes no difference. Blackjack Tar is the most natural-born killer I've ever run across."

"He's an outlaw—" Fargo began.

"No. You're not listening. Tar is more than that. He's got a heart as black as the devil's. Sometimes I think he *is* the devil come to plague us."

"That's the drink talking."

"You don't want to tangle with him and his bunch," Jules said. "You truly don't."

"You're forgetting the pilgrims I have to bring out," Fargo said.

"To hell with them. It was their wagon master's pigheadedness that caught them in the blizzard. Let them fend for themselves until the snow thaws in a few months. Any as are still alive will make it back on their own."

"The army wants me to bring them down."

"Will the army bury you, too, after Tar is done with you?" With a slightly nervous look at the emigrants and soldiers moving about the compound, Jules squared his bony shoulders and moved into the open.

Fargo went with him. "I was hoping you would lead me to them. Harrington says you know right where they are."

"I do, and for your sake, I won't."

"Damn it, Jules. What game are you playing at?"

"Game?" Jules drew up short. "Look at me," he said,

and gestured at himself. "In case you ain't noticed, I'm getting on in years. I don't have too many left, and those I do, I aim to spend taking it as easy as I can."

"Drinking."

"That's mighty strange coming from you. You like whiskey as much as I do."

Fargo couldn't deny that and held his tongue.

"I drink because it makes me feel good, and not much else does these days."

"Helping those people would."

Jules uttered a bark of a laugh. "That might work on greenhorns but not on me. I was long in the tooth before you were born. I learned the hard way that the only life we should give a damn about is our own."

"You don't have to stay once we find them. Take me up and come right back."

"In the first place, I don't even know if we can reach them. When I said they're practically buried in snow, I wasn't joshing. It's up to the canvas in their wagons." Jules took a breath. "In the second place, come right back my ass. It'll take a couple of weeks to reach them, and longer to get back. In the third place, you keep forgetting about Blackjack Tar."

"Maybe it's best I run into him. Maybe I can put an end to it."

"Or maybe he puts an end to you."

Jules marched on to the sutler's.

People they passed took one look and gave him a wide berth. More than a few crinkled their noses.

Fargo trailed along. He was puzzled. This wasn't the Jules he knew. The old trapper had always been feisty and carefree, taking each day as it came, never giving a thought to tomorrow.

The sutler's was crowded with emigrants from the wagon train. They, too, gave way for the reeking scarecrow.

It got to Fargo. "What in hell has happened to you?" he wondered out loud.

"I got old, hoss."

"There has to be more to it."

Once more Jules stopped and looked at him. "No, Skye, there doesn't. It's terrible when time finally catches up with you. I'm not half the man I used to be. My eyes are going. I can't walk as far or ride as far." He hesitated. "And I think I'm sick. Bad sick."

"So you're drinking yourself to death?"

"Go to hell," Jules said, and walked to the counter.

The sutler already had a bottle out and resentment on his face. "You again. I told you to come late in the day. You're bad for my customers."

Jules dug a poke from under his buckskins, plunked down a coin, and snatched the bottle. "I thank you for your hospitality," he said sarcastically.

"At least take a bath, old man," the sutler said. "You wouldn't reek to high heaven."

"When I want your advice I'll ask for it, and I'll never ask for it."

"Keep talking to me like that and that's the last bottle I'll sell you."

Jules muttered and shuffled out.

Fargo debated, and went with him. "If you won't take me, then draw me a map. Or sit me down and give me all the landmarks I need."

"Unless you've been to that exact part of the mountains, it wouldn't do you much good."

"Let me be the judge." Fargo could shave days off his search, and every one counted. Blackjack Tar wasn't the only danger those trapped people were in; starvation and the cold would take a toll.

"I wish you'd leave me be. I don't want anything to do with anybody right now."

"Harrington told me there are kids with that train," Fargo said.

"There's that soft spot of yours."

"I didn't know I had any."

"Usually you're hard as nails. You don't take guff. And you're the meanest son of a bitch alive when your dander is up. But when it comes to women and young'uns, you're as soft as mush."

Fargo thought of Margaret and Jessie.

Jules shook his head. "No, you can fool everyone else but you can't fool me. Women and sprouts are— What do they call it? Your Achilles' foot."

"Achilles' heel."

"Whatever an Achilles is."

"Jules, please."

"No, damn it."

"Why the hell not?"

The old trapper stopped and bowed his head. When he raised it, Fargo was startled to see he was crying.

"You prod and you prod. All right. I'll tell you. And then you'll leave me be or so help me we're quits as pards. Prod me one more time and I'll by God shoot you or gut you. I mean it."

"Listen—" Fargo tried to get in a word.

"No, *you* listen. You wanted to hear and now you will." Jules's voice sank to almost a whisper and he continued to silently weep. "About three months ago, it was, I was up near Badger Peak. There's a stream with beaver, and I laid my traps and got me some prime peltries." A faint smile touched his lips. "It was like the old days. It was glorious." His face clouded. "Then Blackjack Tar got ahold of me."

"What?"

"You heard me. He and his men snuck up on me and jumped me before I could get off a shot. I thought I was done for. I thought he'd stake me out and peel my hide and carve on me like he's done to so many others. But do you know what he did?" Jules gave a short, strange laugh. "He said I wasn't worth the bother. That I was so old and useless, all he was going to do was have some fun and send me on my way." His whole body shook, and he groaned. "Do you want to hear what his idea of fun was?" He didn't wait for Fargo to answer. "He cut my balls off."

12

Fargo's skin crawled. He supposed he'd be more shocked if he hadn't seen the grisly handiwork of Apaches and others. "I'm sorry for you."

"There's more. He cut them off," Jules said, the tears continuing to pour, "and he held them in his hand and laughed at me. And then do you know what he did?"

Fargo shook his head.

"He made me eat them. He stuffed them down my throat and held my mouth shut and I—" Jules stopped and closed his eyes and shook.

"There's no need to go on," Fargo said quietly. He was worry he had pressed him.

"You'll hear it all, damn you. You made me tell you." Jules looked at him in reproach. "He made me eat them. And after I threw up all over myself, he tossed me on my horse and gave it a slap on the rump and sent me on my way. Him and all his men laughing the whole while."

"Damn," Fargo said.

"So you ask me why I won't go back up there? Now you know. You ask me why I'm drinking myself to death? Now you know."

There was nothing Fargo could say so he didn't say a thing.

"I laid up in my cabin for weeks. I healed, but not on the inside. I hated him, wanted him dead. I went looking for him and came across those pilgrims. I also came across sign of Tar and his bunch, and do you know what?"

Fargo shook his head again.

"It scared me so bad, I tucked tail and came straight here. I've never been so afraid. I practically peed myself." Jules regarded the bottle in his hand. "So now if you'll excuse me, I have more drinking and forgetting to do. And don't you dare ask me again to go back up there. I won't, and that's final."

Fargo watched him walk off. "Well, now," he said to himself. He'd have to find the emigrants the hard way. Turning, he went back into the sutler's and bought the supplies he'd need plus extra ammunition and a new whetstone to use for sharpening the Arkansas toothpick. He carried the bundle to the stable and the tack room, where he'd left his saddle. Sinking to a knee, he opened his saddlebags and was transferring the coffee when he heard the slight scrape of a boot or shoe behind him. Thinking it was the corporal he'd seen earlier, he glanced over his shoulder.

It was Fletcher, holding a rifle by the barrel. "I've got you now, you son of a bitch," he made the mistake of saying, and swung.

Fargo ducked and clawed at his Colt. The blow caught him on the shoulder, numbing his arm. He tried to draw but fumbled the revolver and it slipped from his grasp. Before he could grab it with his other hand, a boot slammed into his ribs. He scrambled back but there wasn't room. Another swing of the rifle knocked his hat off. He saw the Henry jutting from the saddle scabbard and lunged for it, only to have a boot meet his face. It dazed him and he fell flat on his belly.

Fingers locked in his hair and his head was wrenched up.

"Can you hear me, you bastard?" Fletcher growled. "Did you think I'd forget about you? That I wouldn't pay you back for what you did?"

Fargo was shaken so violently, his teeth rattled.

"I followed you here. Bet you didn't know that, did you?" Fletcher laughed. "I've been asking around. The great Skye Fargo. Tough hombre. You don't look so tough to me. Fact is, you look like a man who is about to die."

Fargo's vision was clearing and he got his hands under him, only to be rocked by a fist to the jaw. He was cast down and dimly aware that Fletcher had stood.

"I'm going to enjoy this. It's too bad Margaret is still locked up. She'd enjoy it too."

Pain exploded in Fargo's left shoulder. In his right side. He realized Fletcher was beating him to death with the rifle. In desperation he scrambled toward the stalls. Then the side of head felt as if it caved in. Darkness descended. He tried to fight it off and couldn't.

A black well yawned and he pitched into it, thinking this was the end.

The last thing he heard was a yell.

Shaking brought him around. Light shaking on his sore shoulder. The tack room swam and came into focus, as did the concerned face above him.

"You're alive." Colonel Harrington stated the obvious. "Lie still. I've sent for the doctor."

Fargo's tongue felt as if it was covered in wool. He blinked, and hurt, and swallowed, and hurt. "How?" he got out. "What?"

"You owe your life to Corporal Jones here," Harrington said. "He heard a commotion and came in the back and saw a man standing over you with a rifle."

Over the colonel's shoulder, the young corporal who had been sweeping out the stable nodded. "I gave a holler and went for my six-shooter but before I could get it out he ran past me and out the front. The danged flap slowed me."

Most army holsters, Fargo knew, had flaps to protect the revolvers from dust and the elements.

"Who was it?" Harrington asked. "Who did this to you?"

Fargo wet his throat and was about to say when a lieutenant came running into the tack room and said something into the colonel's ear that brought Harrington to his feet.

"I have to go. Jones, look after him until the doctor gets here."

"Yes, sir."

"Wait," Fargo croaked, but Harrington was hurrying out with the lieutenant.

Corporal Jones hunkered. "Is there anything I can get you, mister?"

Fargo's head was pounding. His shoulder hurt to move it and his ribs were on fire. "Whiskey."

"I don't know as I can get you a bottle, sir," Jones said. "We're not allowed to be near the stuff while we're on duty."

"I have some," a familiar voice said, "if you don't mind my spit."

Jules stepped out of the shadows. The new bottle he'd bought was half gone already. He chugged and wiped it with his sleeve and held it out.

"I'm obliged." Fargo tilted the bottle and let the whiskey burn through him. Almost instantly he felt a little better and the pain in his head began to dull.

"I heard a ruckus and came over," Jules said. "Saw him whaling on you with that rifle of his."

Forgetting himself, Fargo glanced up too sharply and was seared by fresh pain. "Why didn't you stop him?"

"I couldn't."

"All you had to do was draw and shoot."

"I thought about it," Jules said. "But if I missed it would have made him mad and he'd have come after me."

"Well, hell, old man," Corporal Jones said. "You ain't nothing but a coward."

Jules colored red and opened his mouth as if to angrily

reply. Instead, he dipped his chin to his chest and said sadly, "I reckon as how you're right, sonny. I didn't used to be but things can change a man."

"Nothing could ever change me that much," Corporal Jones said.

"Don't count on it," Jules said glumly, and walked out. Over his shoulder he said, "You can keep the bottle, pard. It's the least I can do."

Fargo saw his hat and jammed it on his head. He spotted his Colt, too, and shoved it into his holster. Propping a hand under him, he pushed to his feet.

"Whoa, there," Corporal Jones said. "Should you be doing that? The colonel said you're to wait for the sawbones."

Fargo started to push past but caught himself. "You saved my life."

"Shucks, mister," Jones said with a sheepish grin, "I didn't do much but holler. I was half worried that feller would shoot me but he lit out of here quick."

"I still want to thank you. If I can ever return the favor—" Fargo let it go at that. He left the tack room and hurried to the stable entrance.

Quite a commotion was taking place. Emigrants stood around gawking as soldiers dashed every which way, going into buildings, searching every nook and cranny.

Half a dozen uniforms, all officers, were over at the guardhouse. One of them broke away and came toward him, scowling.

"Don't tell me," Fargo said.

"He broke her out," Colonel Harrington said. "From the description it's the same man who attacked you in the stable."

"Fletcher."

"That's who it was? The one you told me about?" Harrington swore. "They can't have gotten far. There hasn't been time."

"If they made it out the gate you'll never see them again," Fargo predicted.

"They might have before the alarm was given," Harrington said. "The sentries had no reason to stop them. People from the wagon train have been coming and going all day."

Fargo needed another swallow.

"Shouldn't you be waiting in the tack room for our doctor?"

"I'm fine," Fargo lied.

"Suit yourself. I need to oversee the search." Harrington hastened toward the gate.

Fargo moved to a water trough and sat on the edge. He was upset with himself. He'd been careless and it had cost him. He should have expected Fletcher to come after Margaret. They were lovers, after all.

A shadow fell across him.

"You're Fargo, I take it?"

The doctor had arrived. He wasn't much past thirty, his uniform no different from any other. The black bag in his left hand gave his true profession away.

"I don't need you," Fargo said.

"How about if I be the judge of that? I'm Captain Griffin, by the way." He leaned closer. "That's a nasty welt you have. It's bled a little. You should let me clean it and patch you up."

"No."

"Why in heaven's name not? Do you enjoy being in pain?"

"I want it to remind me of how stupid I've been."

"What purpose does that serve?"

"I have a score to settle."

"Ah," Griffin said, and studied him. "Something tells me I wouldn't want to be the man you intend to settle it with."

"No," Fargo said. "You wouldn't."

13

Fletcher and Margaret had gotten clean away. The soldiers couldn't find a trace of them.

It didn't surprise Fargo. What did was the invite he got. He was watching troopers drill when the orderly came up and let him know that Colonel Harrington would like the pleasure of his company at the colonel's home at six o'clock for supper.

Fargo wasn't in the mood to be sociable but he told the orderly he'd be there. When it was close to six he changed into his spare buckskin shirt and availed himself of a washbasin to clean the blood from his face.

The colonel lived in one of the few houses at the fort. Only senior officers were afforded that luxury.

Fargo had met Harrington's wife, Ethel, before and she greeted him warmly. A plump, prematurely silver-haired woman with the friendliest smile this side of anywhere, she clasped his hands in hers and warmly escorted him to the parlor.

"It will be another fifteen minutes until we eat," she informed him. "I'm running a little late."

"Take as long as you need," Fargo said. For a home-cooked meal it was worth the wait.

"I'm supposed to tell you that Jessie sends her love. She's staying with Lieutenant Travers and his wife, Polly. They've taken a shine to the child and are considering adopting her."

Fargo was happy for Jessie and said so.

"Here we are," Ethel said.

Fargo was surprised a second time; he wasn't the only one who had been invited.

Colonel Harrington and Captain Griffin were on the settee. Both rose. Harrington pumped his hand, saying, "I believe you two have met."

"That we have," Griffin said, smiling. "Mr. Fargo refused medical treatment, amazingly enough. I trust he won't feel the same about them."

"Them?" Fargo said.

Harrington quickly said, "We'll discuss that later. Right now let's have something to drink to whet our appetite for Ethel's marvelous food."

The colonel wasn't exaggerating.

Fargo was treated to a feast the likes of which he hadn't enjoyed in months. Elk steak, thick and juicy and smothered in onions with a few mushrooms thrown in; whipped potatoes with delicious gravy; succotash, flavored with butter and lightly salted; hot biscuits so soft, he almost felt guilty biting into them; coffee with cream and sugar. For dessert there was apple pie fresh out of the oven; it melted in his mouth.

Harrington and Ethel bantered about army life and how wasn't it a shame that the whites and the red men couldn't get along and the colonel mentioned that he was afraid a lot more blood would be spilled before the West was fully settled.

Fargo didn't like that last part. The settling. The last thing he wanted, the very last thing, was for the wild places to disappear and be replaced by the plow and towns and cities. He knew it was inevitable. Just as every square foot of land between the Atlantic Ocean and the Mississippi River had been devoured by the locusts of civilization, so, too, would every square foot of land between the Mississippi and the Pacific. He liked to think that day was a long ways off. At least, he hoped it didn't happen in his lifetime.

They finished the meal and Harrington suggested they repair to the parlor. No sooner did Fargo make himself comfortable than the colonel and the doctor swapped looks and the colonel cleared his throat.

"So tell me, Skye. When do you plan to head out?"

"At first light," Fargo answered.

"My, that's early," Captain Griffin said. "But I can be ready."

"So that's what this is," Fargo said.

"Hear us out," Colonel Harrington said. "You're well aware of the condition those poor people must be in. They could be freezing to death. They could be suffering from starvation. They could be sick."

"Or they might be perfectly fine," Fargo said. Provided they had plenty of food and could find firewood. He recollected another wagon train that once was stranded for longer than this train had been, and everyone lived through it with nothing worse than a few cases of frostbite.

"They might," Captain Griffin said, "but it's unlikely. And in that regard, my services will be sorely needed."

"I can spare him," Harrington said. "No one is ill except for a few colds, no babies are due, and no one has been wounded since last August."

"It's perfect timing," Griffin said.

"He can minister to them," Harrington said. "He'll take medicines along."

"He'll slow me down," Fargo said.

Griffin's cheeks pinched. "I might not be the best rider in the world but I'm not the worst. I daresay I'll be well able to keep up."

Fargo looked at Harrington. "Have you forgotten about Blackjack Tar?"

Griffin cut in before the colonel could answer. "What

does he have to do with it? I'm not offering my medical services to him."

"He gets his hands on you," Fargo said, "you're as good as dead."

"Why would he kill me for no reason?"

"Because he's Blackjack Tar."

"No one is that coldhearted."

"Hell," Fargo said.

Harrington had a slightly pained expression. "I'm counting on you to keep him safe."

"I don't need protecting," Captain Griffin said. "I might be a physician but I'm also a soldier and I've been trained in the arts of war."

Fargo reminded himself that the doc meant well. "Those arts of yours won't count for much in the wilds."

"Nonsense. I can shoot as well as the next trooper."

"Ever shot at anyone when they were shooting back?"

"Well, no," Griffin said. "The truth is, I've never been in a skirmish."

"Hell," Fargo said.

"You make it sound as if I'd be positively useless, and I resent that."

Fargo looked at Harrington again. "You should reconsider."

"It's my duty," Harrington said. "I'm responsible for their safety and welfare. I have to do something."

"You're sending me."

"I have to do all I can," Harrington amended, "and it's prudent to send the doctor along."

"Did you have this planned when you sent for me?"

"It's *why* I sent for you. Doctors are invaluable on the frontier. I couldn't trust his life with other than the very best."

"I'm not an infant," Captain Griffin said.

"Up in the mountains you will be," Fargo told him.

"Oh, please. I'm a grown man. It's not as if I can't live

off the land. I can hunt. I can cut up a deer. I'll be of great help to you. Wait and see."

Fargo sighed.

"I'm sorry," Colonel Harrington said. "It has to be done or I wouldn't have asked. I have Washington looking over my shoulder, remember?"

Fargo savvied. The loss of so many emigrants wouldn't sit well with the brass. They might need a scapegoat and the colonel was the likeliest.

"I don't suppose I could persuade you to take along half a dozen troopers as well?"

"You're pushing," Fargo said.

"The most experienced men I have," Harrington assured him. "To look after the captain."

"I don't need looking after," Griffin said. "I'm an officer, for God's sake."

Fargo was about to say no. But it hit him that with the boys in blue to see to the sawbones, he'd be free to do as he pleased. "All right."

"Sergeant Petrie will handle the men," Harrington said. "You've met him. And you must agree that he's the—" The colonel stopped. "Wait. What did you just say?"

"They can tag along."

"They can?"

"It's what you want, isn't it?"

"Yes, but—" Harrington tilted his head. "I expected you to take longer to convince. You're giving in too easily."

"You call that easy?" Captain Griffin said.

"You don't know this man like I do," Harrington said. "No one can make him do anything he doesn't want to."

"You're his superior," Griffin said. "You can order him."

Harrington chuckled and said to Fargo, "Do you hear him?"

"He has a lot to learn."

"I'm right here," Captain Griffin said.

Fargo stood and hooked his thumbs in his gun belt. "I

reckon it's settled then. Have the good captain and the rest be at the front gate at sunrise."

The colonel rose and held out his hand. "I will. And thank you."

Griffin stood, too. "I might as well take my leave. I have a lot to prepare."

Fargo took it for granted they would part company at the front door but the physician walked with him toward the stable. "Something on your mind?"

"I'm trying to figure you out."

"I pull on my pants one leg at a time, the same as you do."

"I've never seen the colonel treat anyone with so much deference. What makes you so special?"

Fargo shrugged. "I get the job done."

"So I gather. Before you arrived, the colonel was telling me about the time you and him fought the Apaches. How you saved his patrol."

"I saved my own hide too."

"Modesty ill becomes you."

"Who the hell is being modest?" Fargo retorted. "That's how it was."

"You see me as a hindrance on this rescue mission, don't you?"

"Your words, not mine."

"I promise you I'll hold my own. May the Lord strike me dead if I don't."

"That's just it."

"What is?"

"You ending up dead."

"You're doing wonders for my confidence. If I don't make it back, you have my permission to stomp on my grave and say you told me so."

"Grave, hell," Fargo the said. "The ground is too hard for burying. I'll just piss on you and leave you for the buzzards."

"Surely you're joking?"

"Die and find out."

14

Fargo was up before the crack of dawn. He saddled the Ovaro and brought the stallion out of the stable to a hitch rail. As he was looping the reins a shape detached itself from the darkness. He dropped his hand to his Colt but didn't draw. "You?" he said when he recognized who it was.

"Me," Jules Vallee said. He was mounted on a bay that had seen a lot of years and holding a Sharps in the crook of his elbow.

"What do you think you're doing?"

"Coming along."

"I thought you wanted to spend the rest of your days drunk."

"I thought I did, too," Jules said. "But the booze isn't helping me forget like it's supposed to. I wake up with the sweats, so scared I can't hardly think straight."

"After what you went through—" Fargo said, and let it go at that.

"It turned me yellow," Jules said quietly. "It's gotten so, I'm afeared of my own shadow."

"I wouldn't go that far," Fargo said.

"I am, I tell you," Jules said. "And I'm sick of it. I want to be me again. I want to be able to look at myself and not be sick to my stomach."

"This won't be easy. You said so yourself."

"You reckon I don't know that?" Jules gazed to the

east at the lightening sky. "I have something to prove to myself and this is the only way." He paused. "Besides, you need me to help you find those pilgrims."

"Only if you're sure," Fargo said.

"I've never been more sure of anything in my life."

In the summer the ride from Fort Laramie to the geyser country was pleasant enough; in the winter it was hell.

The cold seeped into their bones before they had gone a mile from the gates, and stayed there. At night they bundled in blankets but it warmed them only a little and by the middle of the night they sometimes woke up freezing with their jaws chattering.

The soldiers, anyway.

Fargo was used to it.

He led them north along the Platte and then along the Sweetwater River to the Wind River Range. South Pass and the Oregon Trail were to the west.

Fargo continued north into the mountains, and from there on he relied on Jules.

Ordinarily, the ruts left by twenty heavy wagons would be enough of a guide. But those ruts were buried under half a foot of snow.

Captain Griffin kept pretty much to himself. Early on he'd tried to engage Fargo in conversation but when he discovered Fargo wasn't much of a talker, he gave it up as a lost cause.

Sergeant Petrie was a solid block of muscle, a career soldier who took his soldiering as seriously as a pastor took the Bible. The five troopers under him were older than average, experienced campaigners who had served long spells on the frontier. During the day they rarely spoke unless spoken to and at night they didn't talk and joke a lot as younger soldiers would.

Now it was a new day and a front was rolling in, the clouds thick and ominous.

Fargo hoped the snow would hold off. He wanted to

get up into the high country and get out again as quickly as practical.

The third morning after they entered the Wind River Range, Fargo brought the Ovaro up alongside the trapper's plodding bay. "How much farther?"

"Miles or days?"

"Both," Fargo said.

The old trapper squinted ahead at jagged white peaks that thrust at the clouds. "As the crow flies, I'd guess not more than fifty miles. On horseback, with all this snow, eight to ten days, I reckon."

"Damn," Fargo said.

"They're up a ways. That Jacob Coarse got it into his head there's a pass over the Tetons."

"How do you know that?"

"He told me."

Fargo almost drew rein. "You talked to him? When?"

"When I first came on them stranded in that meadow. Didn't I mention it? They begged me to go for help."

"Why didn't they send one of their own down sooner?"

"I asked them that," Jules said. "Hell, it's not that hard to find Fort Laramie."

"And?" Fargo prompted when the old trapper didn't go on.

"Jacob Coarse wouldn't let anyone leave. He said they had to stick together no matter what."

"The damned fool."

"To tell the truth, they didn't impress me much. Farmers, mostly, and a few city folk. They were bound to get lost."

"So they stay stranded when they don't have to be."

"Part of it is they refuse to leave their wagons. Everything those people own is on their Conestogas. They're fearful it will get taken if they leave it untended."

"What's more important?" Fargo grumbled. "Their china and grandfather clocks or their lives?"

"You know how some folks are," Jules said with a sigh. "They're more attached to things than they are to breathing."

"So much for talking them into leaving their wagons up there until spring."

Jules laughed. "Not likely. They'd as soon chop off an arm and a leg."

Fargo gazed at the swirling clouds. "What we need is a warm spell."

"What we have is winter."

As if to bring that point home, large flakes began to fall. Only a few but it portended worse to come.

"Wonderful," Fargo said.

They hadn't gone much farther when they came on fresh tracks.

"What do you make of those?" Jules asked.

Fargo drew rein and bent from the saddle. A pair of riders—on shod horses—had come from the southeast and gone off toward the northwest. Judging by the little amount of snow that had filled the tracks, it couldn't have been more than half an hour ago. He related as much.

"Who in hell would be heading up into the high country in weather like this?"

"In the same direction as the stranded wagon train," Fargo had noticed.

"Could be a couple of them tried to make it to the fort and turned back."

"Could be," Fargo said, although his gut instinct told him that wasn't the case.

"If they stop we might run into them," Jules mentioned. "Then we'll know."

They climbed, and the snow thickened.

Fargo marveled that the pilgrims had made it so far. Lacking a trail, they'd had to choose the easiest route by sight, avoiding steep grades and the thickest timber and deadfalls. They must have pushed their teams to try to make it over the mountains before the first snow. Little did they know that other than South Pass and another pass nearly a hundred miles to the north, there was no way over the Divide. Not for wagons, anyhow.

The snow had turned the greens and browns to stark white. White peaks, white slopes, white trees, white ground. It was picturesque but treacherous. The snow hid obstacles that would otherwise be avoided. And it made even the slightest of slopes slippery for beast and man.

The normally dry air wasn't. Thick with moisture, it made breathing at high altitudes harder. They weren't so high yet that it would pose a problem but it was something to keep in mind.

Fargo didn't resent the snow. Not like others he knew. Some scouts refused to head out into the wilds in the winter if a lot of snow had fallen. The odds of making it back were slimmer. A man had to know exactly what he was doing and even then there were no guarantees.

"Do you smell that, pard?" Jules asked.

Fargo had been so caught up in thought, he hadn't. He sniffed and said, "Smoke."

"That pair must have made camp."

It was early yet but that meant nothing. Fargo rose in the stirrups but couldn't spot the telltale tendrils. "They can't be far ahead."

They rode on, the clomp of their hooves muffled by the white blanket. Occasionally clumps of snow fell from trees, showering them.

The tracks entered a belt of pines.

Out of habit Fargo rode with his hand on his Colt. "Tell the troopers not to make any noise," he said quietly over his shoulder, and Jules passed it on to Captain Griffin in a whisper.

The orange flames were easy to spot.

Fargo drew rein and the others followed suit. Dismounting, he handed the reins to Jules and glided forward.

The pair had camped in a small clearing. Their horses were tied and a coffeepot had been put on. But there was no sign of the riders.

Fargo squatted to wait. It could be they were gathering firewood. They wouldn't have gone far.

When they emerged, their arms laden with broken branches, he gave a start. He supposed he shouldn't be surprised but he was. Drawing the Colt, he cocked it and moved into the open. They were talking and looking at one another and didn't see him until he said, "Fancy meeting you here."

Fletcher and Margaret froze.

"You!" she blurted.

"And friends," Fargo said. He gave a loud whistle.

Fletcher glanced at the stock of a rifle jutting from a scabbard on a sorrel.

"Try for it," Fargo urged. "Give me an excuse."

"The colonel sent you after us," Fletcher said.

"You won't believe this," Fargo said, "but we found you by accident."

"Can we set down this firewood?" Margaret asked, hefting her burden.

"No."

Out of the pines came Jules and Captain Griffin and Sergeant Petrie and the five soldiers. Petrie promptly drew his sidearm and ordered his men to do the same.

"Now you can set the firewood down," Fargo said. He walked around behind them and relieved Fletcher of his six-shooter and Margaret of a Smith & Wesson she'd acquired somewhere.

Fletcher was boiling mad and trying hard to contain himself. "I thought we'd gotten clean away."

"Of all the places in the world," Fargo said, "why in hell did you come way up here?"

"To join up with Blackjack Tar," Margaret said. "Why else?"

"You killed our other friends," Fletcher said.

Jules said, "Blackjack Tar ain't anyone's friend. He's as liable to kill you as anything."

"Blackjack would never harm a hair on our heads," Margaret declared.

"And why's that, missy?" Jules asked.

"Because I'm his sister."

15

Margaret Tar. Fargo would never have suspected that. It explained a lot.

Evening was setting. The snow had tapered to flurries. Fletcher and Margaret sat with their hands bound behind their backs, Fletcher still simmering, Margaret acting as if it was perfectly natural for her to be covered by two of the troopers.

"This is a stroke of luck," Sergeant Petrie commented as the coffeepot was being passed around. "I should send them back under guard in the morning."

"We take them with us," Fargo said.

The sergeant shook his head. "They killed Trooper Hayes. They have to answer for it."

"We don't split up."

Petrie stared at the pair and tapped his tin cup with a thick finger. "My orders are to escort you to the Coarse wagon train and assist you in getting them down the mountains to safety. I can do that with three men as well as five."

"And if her brother shows up?" Jules said with a nod at Margaret. "Three of you ain't hardly enough."

"Two less won't make that much of a difference," Petrie argued.

Fargo was dead set against it. "I'd take it as a favor if you didn't."

Captain Griffin settled the matter by saying, "We'll do as he wants, Sergeant, and that's final."

"Yes, sir," Petrie said unhappily.

Margaret had listened to every word and was grinning.

"What's so funny, girlie?" Jules asked.

"I'm not no girl. I'm a full-grown woman," she shot back. "And what's funny is what my brother will do when he gets hold of you. He won't like you taking me prisoner. He won't like it at all."

Petrie said to Griffin, "All the more reason for me to send them to the fort. Blackjack Tar won't know they've been taken into custody."

"That's a good point," Margaret said. "You should listen to him, Captain."

Fargo was puzzled. It made no sense for her to want to be taken to Fort Laramie. They wouldn't hang her. Woman were rarely hanged. But she'd likely spend a good many years behind bars.

"Cat got your tongue?" Jules said to Fletcher. "You haven't given your two cents."

"I get the chance," Fletcher growled, "I'll kill every last one of you."

"That's what I like to see," Jules said. "Brotherly love."

Fargo snorted.

"You won't think it's so hilarious when you meet *my* brother," Margaret boasted. "You'll die slow and horrible and begging for mercy."

"That's enough of that kind of talk," Captain Griffin said. "It's not fit for a lady."

Margaret Tar laughed. "Who the hell are you talking to? I haven't ever been a *lady*. I drink like a man and cuss like a man and kill like a man. And yes, I screw like a man, too."

"Such language," Jules said.

Margaret winked at Fargo. "Tell them how I am. Tell them how it really is."

"She's a bitch," Fargo said.

"And proud of it," Margaret said, her eyes twin points of vicious glee. "I liked killing that old granny and that old man. I like killing, period."

"You're not in your right mind," Captain Griffin remarked.

"Wretch," Margaret said. "Thinking everyone should think as you do. Some of us won't be chained by rules and such."

"Now you're talking nonsense," Captain Griffin said. "No one has put chains on you."

Margaret bent toward him. "I could tell you things that would curl your hair. You wouldn't—"

"Enough," Fletcher said. She looked at him and he said, "I mean it."

Fargo was impressed that she listened. "I was wondering which of you is worse. Now I know."

"I don't listen to him out of fear," Margaret said. "I do it out of love."

"Hell," Jules said. "I doubt you know the meaning of the word."

"Why? Because I kill and steal?"

"I said enough," Fletcher warned her.

"And you want to take these two with us?" Sergeant Petrie said to Griffin. "With all due respect, sir, we'll have to watch them every second. At least two of my men will have them under constant guard. We might as well send them to the fort."

"No is no. Not another word," Captain Griffin said.

Margaret stared intently at Fargo. "So tell me, handsome. How does it feel to be chasing your tail?"

"How do you mean?" Fargo asked.

Fletcher turned on her, glowering. "Damn it to hell.

Give it away and your brother will take a bullwhip to you, sister or not."

"Blackjack would never lay a finger on me," Margaret said. "Besides, a gal has to have her fun."

"That's all you ever want to do."

"Now, now," Margaret said.

"Rabid coyotes," Jules said. "The pair of them."

Fargo wasn't so sure. They were hiding something. He couldn't imagine what. "Both of you are done talking for a while."

"Or what?" Margaret rejoined. "You'll pistol-whip us? You would, wouldn't you? The good captain wouldn't, me being a lady and all. But you, you're more like us than you'll own up to."

Fargo put his hand on his Colt and smirked and had the satisfaction of seeing her blanch.

"I reckon I'll sleep with one eye open tonight," Jules remarked.

"You don't need to worry," Sergeant Petrie said. "We'll tie their legs and gag them until morning. They're not going anywhere."

"I broke out of your guardhouse, didn't I?" Margaret boasted.

"With his help," Petrie said with a gesture at Fletcher. "This time he'll be as trussed up as you."

"Gloat while you can," Margaret said. "But you don't know everything."

"For the last goddamn time," Fletcher said, "shut the hell up."

The snow finally stopped but the wind picked up. Once the sun was swallowed by the mountains, the temperature plummeted.

Fargo didn't object when the troopers added wood to make the fire larger and warmer. He doubted any hostiles were abroad. Not in that weather.

Jules Vallee draped a blanket over his slim shoulders and pulled it tight around him. "You get my age, the cold bothers you more."

"My brother will see to it you don't get any older," Margaret predicted.

"About him," Jules said. "What made him how he is? You, too, for that matter? How can you go around killing folks and not give a damn?"

"Why should we?" Margaret replied. "They're strangers. They're nothing to us."

"They're people, for God's sake."

Margaret looked at him in scorn. "You want to understand us—is that it? We have to have a reason so you can sleep better at night."

"It's not natural," Jules said.

"Tell me, old man," Margaret said. "I hear tell you were a trapper once. One of the best of the beaver men. How many of them did you kill?"

"Beaver?" Jules shrugged. "I never counted 'em. In the early years, before most of the streams were trapped out, I probably caught three to four hundred a year. My best year was close to five."

"So all told," Margaret said, "you killed thousands of beavers in your time."

"I reckon. So what?"

"Do you regret it?"

"Why would I? I was earning a living, same as a lot of men. And they were beaver. They were no more to us than the deer we eat for supper or the buffalo we shot."

"There you have it," Margaret said.

"Have what?"

"That's exactly what people are to my brother and me. They're deer. They're buffalo. They're beaver. Doing them in is no different to us than killing animals is to you."

"You're"—Jules seemed to search for the right way to say it—"sick in the head."

"By how you think. Not by how we think."

One of the troopers covering them said, "Can we shut her up now, Sarge?"

"Good idea, Benton. Tie their legs and gag them. And if they give you trouble, no need to be nice about it."

"You'll get yours, blue belly," Fletcher said.

Fargo was grateful for the silence but it didn't last long. He had gotten up to arch his back and stretch his legs when a shot cracked in the distance and echoed off the peaks, seeming to come from everywhere at once.

"Someone's shooting." A soldier stated the obvious.

"At this time of night?" Petrie said.

"Maybe it's the pilgrims," another trooper said.

"Could be it's Blackjack Tar," Jules put in.

If it wasn't for the snow, Fargo would saddle the Ovaro and scout around. But at night he would be asking for a fall and risk the Ovaro breaking a leg.

"By tomorrow night we should be at the wagons," Jules said. "The morning after at the latest if something holds us up."

"Like Blackjack Tar," Private Benton said.

"He shows his face, I'll put a slug in it," Sergeant Petrie said.

Fargo saw Margaret glare at him, then glance over at her saddle. It was next to Fletcher's and had been left untended. On an impulse he went over, hunkered, and opened her saddlebags.

Almost immediately Margaret started making angry sounds and made as if to wriggle toward him.

"What's gotten into her?" Jules wondered.

The first saddlebag was crammed with money and jewelry: rings, necklaces, bracelets, several pocket watches, an ivory stickpin, and more. A poke bulged with coins and there was a wad of paper money.

One of the soldiers whistled. "Will you look at it all."

"Ill-gotten gains," Jules said.

"Evidence," Captain Griffin said. "I'm confiscating it and turning it over to Colonel Harrington."

Fargo reached into the second saddlebag and pulled out a cloth bundle wrapped with twine. He set it down, undid the twine, and opened the cloth. Inside were a dozen or more irregular patches of . . . something.

"What are those?" Sergeant Petrie asked.

The old trapper bent down, and stiffened. "God help us," he said. "That's human skin."

16

Captain Griffin, thinking it was a joke, snorted and said, "You expect us to believe that?"

"I'm telling you," Jules said. "I've cured more hides than you can count. Not just beaver. And I saw some cured human skin once." He pointed at the collection. "It looked just like these."

A couple of the troopers appeared fit to be sick.

Fargo went around the fire and undid Margaret Tar's gag. "I knew a lady once who collected buttons," he said. "And another who collected silver spoons."

Margaret laughed.

"I knew a gent who collected books and another who collected knives."

"My brother collects skin," Margaret said.

"They're not yours?" Jules asked.

"I like to hold them and run my hands over them so he let me have a few."

"A few?" Captain Griffin said, horrified.

"Look at you," Margaret said. "All you blue bellies. Pale as bedsheets. And you call yourselves fighting men? Hell, you're a bunch of babies."

Fargo held the gag out. "Open," he said.

"I will not."

"Then I'll club you and do it anyhow."

Sheer hate twisted her face as Margaret spat, "I can't wait for my brother to start in on you. I'm going to ask him to take his time and make you cry and blubber like some do."

"Wishful thinking," Fargo said. "Now open wide." She glared but she didn't try to bite his fingers off. He retied the gag tighter than it had to be.

"Human skin," Sergeant Petrie said. "The tales they tell about Blackjack Tar must be true."

"Don't let it get to you," Captain Griffin advised. "He's a man like any other."

Fargo remembered saying the same thing to the captain back at the fort.

"No man I know would do such a thing, sir," Private Benton said.

"Apaches do worse," Sergeant Petrie said, and nodded at the bundle. "We should burn those."

"Aren't they, what did the captain call it, evidence?" Jules asked.

"It's evidence we can do without," Captain Griffin said in disgust. "It's hideous. Barbaric." He stared pointedly at Margaret. "Only a sick person could do such a thing."

It made no difference to Fargo but he could tell the soldiers were spooked. With a shrug, he dropped the bundle into the flames. The cloth sputtered and caught and soon a new odor filled the air.

"God," a trooper said, and covered his nose and mouth.

Margaret laughed through her gag. She thought it was hysterical.

Not an hour later everyone turned in.

Fargo was glad. He took the first watch and sat sipping coffee and savoring the quiet.

Once he heard a wolf but other than that the wilds were unnaturally still. Most times of the year there'd be coyotes yipping and maybe a fox would call out or a mountain lion would scream.

Not tonight.

Fargo thought about Jacob Coarse. No one with a lick of sense would take a passel of inexperienced men and women and their children up into the Rockies in the middle of winter. It made him wonder how long Coarse had been guiding wagon trains.

Along about midnight Fargo woke Petrie. He was still wide awake and figured it would take a while to drift off. Yet he'd hardly closed his eyes and he was under and slept soundly until his inner clock woke him at the crack of the new day.

It was cold as hell.

The troopers stamped their feet and held their hands to the fire to get their circulation going.

Jules nipped from a flask.

Fargo removed the gags from the prisoners and untied their feet so they could stand and stamp, too.

Fletcher was in a foul mood. "I'll remember you for this," he grumbled.

"There won't be anything left to remember after my brother gets through with him," Margaret said with sadistic glee.

"Did you two want something to eat or would you rather go hungry all day?" Fargo asked. That shut them up until after breakfast.

With Jules in the lead and on the lookout for landmarks, they pressed on. The old trapper talked to himself as they went, saying things like, "I remember that peak." Or, "I recollect that switchback."

Fargo remembered the shot from the night before and kept watch for hoofprints.

Twice they came on wolf sign, enough to suggest a pack was in the area. Late in the morning they found where a lone elk had plowed through the snow.

At noon Fargo called a halt. Their animals needed the rest. He took pemmican from his saddlebags and bit and chewed while contemplating the white expanse spread before them. Some would call it a wonderland. He called it white death.

Margaret walked over, a trooper a few steps behind with his revolver out.

"Aren't you going to share?" she asked, indicating the pemmican.

"Not with you."

"You are one mean son of a bitch. Have your fun while you can."

"That works both ways." Fargo bit off another piece and made a show of chewing.

Instead of becoming angry, Margaret grinned. "You won't believe this but I like you."

"You're right. I don't."

"I'm serious. You're almost as mean as me and my brother. I admire that."

"Coming from anyone else I'd be flattered."

"Be nice."

Fargo snorted.

"What do you have against us? Sure, we kill folks, but otherwise we're not as terrible as people make us out to be."

"Where to start?" Fargo said. "How about your brother and his skin collection?"

Margaret shrugged. "He likes skin. There are things you like a lot. Whiskey, as I recall. And you sure as hell are fond of coffee. You drink it by the gallon."

Fargo stared at her. So did the trooper.

"What?" Margaret said.

"If you can't see it," Fargo said, "you have blinders on."

"There are lines people shouldn't cross, lady," the trooper said.

"Lines other people make up," Margaret said. "My brother and me do pretty much as we please."

"I can't wait to meet him," Fargo said.

"Admit it," Margaret said. "You're as scared of him as everyone else."

"He likes that, doesn't he?" Fargo asked. "People being afraid of him?"

"Who wouldn't? I've seen grown women near faint at the mention of his name and grown men near wet themselves." Margaret cackled.

"Loco must run in your family," Fargo said.

Margaret stopped laughing and frowned. "You know about our pa, then?"

"He's loco too?"

"So folks said. He's why my brother and me came west. All those people whispering behind our backs and pointing at us. Just because the state of Tennessee saw fit to put our pa in a sanitarium. All he did was slit our ma's throat and eat a couple of her fingers."

"He did what?" The soldier gasped.

Margaret nodded. "You'd've thought Pa ate her down to the bone, the way everyone carried on."

"Your pa is still there?" Fargo asked.

"Last we knew. He hated it. Hated that they kept him in one of those jackets where you can't move your arms. They claimed they had to do it because he was a danger to himself and others."

"Hard to imagine."

Margaret nodded. "He'd never killed anybody before Ma. Likely as not he wouldn't have done in anyone else, yet they wouldn't release him."

"The bastards," Fargo said.

"That's how Blackjack felt. He wanted to march into that sanitarium and kill every last one of the sons of bitches. Then one day he actually got them to take that jacket off Pa, and what do you think Pa did when Blackjack walked into the room? Pa tried to bite his fingers, is what. So they put the jacket back on Pa and Blackjack said to hell with it, and to hell with him, and to hell with Tennessee, and here we are."

"Taking up where your pa left off."

Margaret gave him a sharp look. "You've been poking fun at me this whole time, haven't you?"

Before Fargo could reply, Jules hurried over, clapped his shoulder, and pointed.

"Do you see what I see?"

Fargo swore, annoyed at himself. He'd been so caught up in Margaret's tale, he hadn't noticed gray wisps rising to the slate sky approximately a quarter mile higher up.

"I do declare," Margaret said. "Smoke, or I'm the queen of England."

"It's too soon to be the pilgrims," Jules said. "We're nowhere near the meadow where their wagons are stuck."

That narrowed the prospects.

"Maybe it's Blackjack Tar," Fargo said.

Margaret brightened and took a step as if she was about to go running off up the mountain.

"Stay right where you are, lady," the trooper warned, training his revolver.

"Would you shoot sweet little me in the back?" Margaret taunted.

"I've never shot a female," the trooper said, "but for you I'd make an exception."

"Remind me to have my brother pry your eyes out with a fork," Margaret said.

"God," the trooper said.

Captain Griffin and Sergeant Petrie joined them.

"I'll take two men and go have a look, sir," the sergeant proposed.

"I'll go," Fargo said. "You have prisoners to watch."

"It doesn't take all of us."

"These two it does."

"Why, darling," Margaret said playfully, "I thank you for the compliment. If my hands weren't tied, I'd kiss you."

"Crazy bitch," the trooper said.

"None of that in front of the lady, Private Cooper," Captain Griffin scolded.

"Oh, sugar," Margaret said impishly, "I lost any hope of being a lady the day my third cousin on my ma's side took me out behind the woodshed."

"We'll let Mr. Fargo go," Captain Griffin said.

Fargo was almost grateful for the smoke. To get away from Margaret for a while would be a treat. He forked leather and reined around. "If I'm not back by sundown, odds are I won't be coming back at all."

"So long as it's not an ambush you'll be fine," Jules said.

"And if it is," Sergeant Petrie said, "we'll bury your remains."

"If we can find them," Jules said.

17

The climb was treacherous. The snow made footing uncertain. Twice the Ovaro slipped, and that was before they came to a boulder field.

Fargo drew rein. White mounds covered the entire slope. Under each was a boulder. He debated going around. He'd lose a lot of time but it was safer for the Ovaro. The hell of it was, the smoke wasn't that far above the boulders.

With an oath, Fargo reined to the left. He came to thick forest and started up again.

The pines, the spruce, the oaks were heavy with their burdens. Branches sagged, some on the verge of breaking.

Now and again one did. He'd hear a loud crack and a crash and snow would rain.

Otherwise the forest was uncommonly quiet. Few birds warbled. A jay squawked, letting everything know an intruder was abroad. Few animals were around to hear. Squirrels were snug in their nests. Rabbits were in their burrows. Deer were in the deep thickets where the meat-eaters would find it harder to stalk them. The meat-eaters were waiting for night to come out and prowl.

Fargo's nose tingled with each inhale. His ears hurt, too. He had to be careful not to get frostbit.

Loose snow constantly sifted from the trees. Sometimes it landed on his hat and shoulders. Sometimes it came down on the back of his neck and a bolt of cold shot through him. He didn't have gloves and could sorely use a pair.

As he neared the spot where the smoke came from, Fargo swept his bearskin coat back so he could draw that much faster.

He'd traded for the coat a month or so ago. A fellow scout took a Sioux arrow in the gut, and lived. The miracle convinced him that scouting wasn't for him anymore, and he sold or traded off things he didn't care to take back east.

Fargo got the coat for a compass he never used and a spyglass.

He could use the spyglass now. He had to remember to buy a new one.

A familiar odor gave his nose new cause to tingle. Fargo reined up. If he was close enough to smell the smoke from the campfire, he was close enough to walk. Climbing down, he shucked the Henry, levered a cartridge into the chamber, and looped the Ovaro's reins around a limb.

Moving quietly was no problem. The snow muffled every step. And there were so many trees he had plenty of cover.

He didn't know what he expected. Blackjack Tar, maybe. Or some of Tar's cutthroats. Or a hunting party sent out by the wagon train.

He certainly didn't expect to see two women who couldn't be much over twenty seated on either side of a fire sipping tea.

Fargo watched and listened but they didn't say anything. They looked glum and anxious. One had a rifle against her leg. The other didn't appear to be armed. Both wore britches instead of dresses, including hats and scarves and gloves.

Cradling the Henry to show he was friendly, Fargo

strode from concealment and plastered a smile on his face. "Ladies," he said. "How do you do?"

Both shot to their feet.

The one with the rifle snatched it up and pointed it at him. Red hair spilled from under her hat, and she had the most marvelous green eyes. At the moment they were pools of fear mixed with anger. "Hold it right there."

The other woman was blond. She had an oval face and pouty lips and a kinder expression. "Oh!" was all she said.

Fargo stopped and went on smiling. "You're a long ways from anywhere," he remarked, and introduced himself.

"I'm Josephine," said the one with the kind face and full lips. "I'm pleased to meet you."

"What in hell are you doing?" the redhead snapped.

"He's friendly," Josephine said.

"He's one of them. He has to be."

"We don't know that, Hortense."

Hortense fixed a bead on Fargo's chest. "Who else would he be? That damned Tar has men everywhere."

Fargo chuckled. "I'm not one of them. I'm a scout. I'm here with some soldiers to find a wagon train that got stranded. Would you be part of it?"

Josephine clasped her hands together. "Did you hear him?"

"I heard his damn lies," Hortense said. To Fargo she replied, "You might be able to fool her but you can't fool me. You're one of them. I feel it in my bones."

"You need new bones," Fargo said. He went to lower the Henry and heard the click of her rifle hammer.

"Mister, I will by God shoot you dead where you stand if you so much as move a muscle."

"Hortense," Josephine said.

"I mean it," Hortense said. "I won't let him or anyone else stop us. We're getting out of here. Out of these damnable mountains and away from Blackjack Tar and away from Jacob Coarse."

"You're with the train?" Fargo said. "I was told it wasn't close by."

"How would you know that," Hortense smirked, "unless you were one of them?"

"A trapper by the name of Jules Vallee is with us," Fargo said. "He stopped and talked to your wagon boss on his way out of the mountains."

"Now I know you're lying," Hortense said. "I don't remember no trapper ever showing up at our camp."

"I don't, either," Josephine said, sounding disappointed.

"Maybe you weren't there at the time," Fargo said. "Maybe you were off fetching water or firewood or who the hell knows? It's easy enough to prove who I am. Follow me down a ways and you can talk to the soldiers yourselves."

"Oh, sure," Hortense said. "We let down our guard and you jump us. How dumb do you reckon we are?"

Fargo frowned. He couldn't blame them for being suspicious. But he didn't like having that rifle pointed at him. Especially with her as anxious as he was. All her finger had to do was curl a little tighter and the rifle would go off.

"I think we can trust him," Josephine said.

"You think you can trust everybody," Hortense said. "You trusted Jacob Coarse, didn't you? And look where that got us."

"You signed on the same as me," Josephine said.

"Only because you were so set on it." Hortense swore, then said bitterly, "Oregon Country. The land of milk and honey. Where we could start a new life and live happily ever after." She shook her head. "You always did live in the clouds."

Josephine looked as if she might burst into tears. "That was uncalled for. We talked it over before we ever bought our wagon and joined the train. It was your decision as much as it was mine."

"Hell," Hortense said. "I always do whatever you want. You know that."

"Don't blame this on me," Josephine said, a tear trickling down her cheek. "How was I to know it would turn out as it has?"

"That damned Jacob Coarse," Hortense said. "Him and his shorter route."

Fargo was being ignored. Clearing his throat, he said, "Remember me?"

"What do you want, outlaw?" Hortense said.

"I told you I'm a scout."

"Mister, you could tell me the sky was up and the ground is down and I wouldn't believe you. For all we know, you're the one who's to blame for those who have disappeared."

"I didn't think of that," Josephine said.

"You've lost me," Fargo said.

Hortense took a step toward him, her cheeks twitching with anger. "Pretend you don't know."

"People have vanished from our wagon train," Josephine explained. "Seven so far but there's likely to be more."

"People don't just vanish," Fargo said.

"These have," Josephine insisted. "There are never any tracks to tell us where they went."

"In all this snow?" Fargo said skeptically.

"One was a man who went to fetch firewood," Josephine said. "He never came back. Mr. Coarse and some of the other men followed his tracks into the woods. They said the tracks came to a stop and then there was nothing."

"That's impossible," Fargo said. "Whoever told you that was lying."

Hortense raised her rifle so her sights were centered on

108

his face and not his chest. "You know what happened to him, don't you? Him and the others?"

Josephine said, "I thought they must be mistaken somehow. But then Mrs. Carmody disappeared. She went to the stream and never came back. I saw her tracks myself. They led to the stream and stopped and that was it. It was like she up and floated off into the air."

"People don't float," Fargo said. The only thing he could think of was that the missing people had been taken and the snow brushed clean of tracks with a tree limb or some other way.

"All that is fine and dandy," Hortense said to Josephine, "but it's this so-called scout we have to deal with now. I say we shoot him."

"We don't know he's not who he says he is."

"Goddamn you."

"Please. No more swearing. You know I don't like it when you swear."

It struck Fargo that these two were acting like a married couple. "Tell me this much," he prompted. "Where are you two headed?"

"I thought we already did say," Josephine said.

"We're getting the hell out of here before we disappear too," Hortense said.

Josephine nodded. "We hear tell Fort Bridger is to the south and Fort Laramie is farther east. We haven't quite made up our minds which to head for." She let out a sad sigh. "We left our wagon and all our possessions behind. It was the hardest thing I've ever had to do."

"It was either that or disappear like all the others," Hortense said.

"Coarse didn't try to stop you from leaving?" Fargo asked. Most wagon masters—the good ones, anyhow—wouldn't let anyone up and leave.

"We never told him we were going," Josephine said. "He'd try to stop us like he did some of the others."

"Who does he think he is, anyhow?" Hortense said. "Bossing people around like he does. Acting like God Almighty all the time." She did more swearing. "All he did was get us stranded."

"I'm glad to be shed of him but I'm not glad to be shed of our wagon and our effects," Josephine said.

From out of the trees behind them, a voice said, "Is that any way to talk about a man who only has your best interests at heart?"

Both women turned as four men strode into the clearing.

"Miss me?" one of the men said.

18

The man who had spoken was as tall as Fargo and as broad across the shoulders but there any resemblance ended. He had a square face with tufts of stubble, a bulbous nose, and big ears. Beetling brows and dark eyes added to his brutish aspect. He held a Spencer rifle and had a six-shooter on his hip. "Did you miss me?" he asked a second time when the shocked women didn't respond.

Hortense recovered first. She pointed her rifle at him and he stopped. "What the hell are you doing here, Coarse?"

Fargo studied him. So this was the wagon master who had stranded his wagons where they had no business being in the dead of winter.

"Is that any way to talk to me, gal?" Jacob Coarse said. "After we came all this way to fetch you back."

"You did what?" Josephine said.

"I couldn't let you traipse off like you done," Coarse said. "It's not safe for you to be wandering these mountains."

"We're not wandering," Hortense spat. "We're leaving them for good and there's nothing you can do to stop us."

"You hear her, boys?" Coarse said, with a glance and a grin at the others.

Fargo studied them, too. They bore the stamp of the same brute mold. He took an immediate dislike to all four, especially Coarse. "The ladies are free to do whatever they want," he interjected.

Jacob Coarse looked at him and blinked as if he suddenly realized Fargo was there. "Who the hell are you?"

"He says he's a scout," Josephine said.

"Likely story," Coarse said.

"He says he's with soldiers."

"What?" Coarse stiffened and the other three reacted similarly.

"You heard her," Fargo said. "Colonel Harrington at Fort Laramie heard you were stranded and sent soldiers to escort you down."

"How in hell did he hear about us?" Coarse asked. Before Fargo could answer, he scowled and said, "Wait. Don't tell me. That old trapper who paid us a visit."

"Jules Vallee," Fargo said.

Coarse nodded. "That was his handle. He never said anything about heading to Fort Laramie."

"You're lucky he did," Fargo said.

"Lucky," Coarse said. He didn't look pleased about it. Nor did the others. "Where are these soldiers?"

"Down the mountain a little ways," Fargo said.

A lean man with a scar on his left cheek swallowed and said as if to himself, "They'll come to the meadow. They'll help get the pilgrims out."

"Isn't that what you want?" Fargo said.

"Of course he does," Jacob Coarse said. "It's what we all want. It just comes as a surprise, is all. We didn't know anyone knew we were missing."

"I'll go fetch the soldiers," Fargo offered, but stopped when Hortense swung her rifle toward him.

"Hold on. You still haven't convinced me you're telling the truth. For all we know, you ride with Blackjack Tar."

"Say, that's right," Coarse said. "This could be a trick."

Fargo had had enough. He was tired of having her rifle pointed at him, and tired of so much stupid. In the blink of an eye he took a step and pressed the Henry's muzzle to

112

Hortense's chin one-handed. His right hand was at his holster, and when one of the men with Coarse shifted toward him and went to level a rifle, he drew and cocked the Colt.

The man turned to stone.

"Jesus!" the one with the scar blurted. "I never saw anyone slick leather so fast."

"The next person points a gun at me," Fargo warned, "takes lead."

"I knew you ride with Tar," Hortense spat.

"Let down the hammer," Fargo said, and when she reluctantly complied, he told her, "Now set it down, nice and slow."

"In the snow?"

"Do it."

Her lips a slit, Hortense obeyed.

Fargo addressed Jacob Coarse. "Now you and your friends."

"Damn it," Coarse said. "You ask a lot."

"Who's asking?" Fargo said.

They didn't like it but the Colt was a great persuader.

"I'll be back with the troopers in a couple of hours," Fargo said. "Stay put until they get here." He began to back off.

"Wait," Josephine said. "Take us with you. Hortense and me."

Both Hortense and Jacob Coarse said, "What?" at the same time.

Heedless of the Colt and the Henry, Josephine put her hand on Fargo's arm.

"Please. I wouldn't feel safe. We left the wagon train to get away from this man." Josephine nodded at the wagon master.

"Silly talk," Coarse said. "What did I ever do to you?"

"Besides strand us in the mountains?" Josephine retorted. "Besides insist we not try to make our way out until the weather thaws? Despite do nothing when our people disappear?"

"Damn, girl," Coarse said. "You make me sound next to worthless."

"If the shoe fits," Josephine said.

"What about your friend?" Fargo asked. "How does she feel?"

Hortense answered for herself. "I won't shoot you in the back, if that's what you're afraid of. If there really are soldiers, I'll be damn glad."

One of the men started to say something and Jacob Coarse made a sharp gesture, silencing him. Coarse then said, "If they're going, we'll go, too. Just to make sure you are who you say you are."

That was fine by Fargo. He'd rather have them all where he could see them. "Fetch your horses. Your rifles go in the scabbards. You ride in front of me until we get there. Once we head out, no one turns back."

"Who do you think you are?" the man with the scar said. "Bossing us around."

Fargo pointed the Colt at him. "You want to go, you do as I say."

"You heard the man," Jacob Coarse said, and was the first to turn and walk into the trees. The rest trailed after him, the man with the scar glaring.

"You'd better watch Treach," Josephine said. "He's likely to stab you in the back if you give him half the chance."

"He has a knife?" Fargo hadn't seen a sheath on the man's hip.

"Up his sleeve," Josephine said. "I've seen him cut meat with it."

"I'm obliged for the warning."

Josephine had nice teeth. "We can't let anything happen to you. You're our best bet of making it out of the mountains. Not just Hortense and me, but everyone with the wagon train."

"I won't believe there are soldiers until I see them with my own eyes," Hortense said.

"She's suspicious by nature," Josephine said.

"I noticed," Fargo said. He gathered up the guns and laid them on a patch of dry ground near the fire. Squatting, he watched the woods, alert in case Coarse and his bunch should try something.

Josephine hunkered beside him. "I'm sorry how everyone is treating you."

"Oh, please," Hortense said. She had folded her arms and was tapping her foot.

"She's just looking after me," Josephine said.

"Sure she is," Fargo replied, and thought of something he'd like to know. "Those men with Coarse. Have they been with him since the beginning?"

"Why, no," Josephine said. "They didn't sign on in Saint Joseph, Missouri, like the rest of us. They didn't join until Fort Laramie."

"You don't say."

"They've been like four peas in a pod ever since," Hortense threw in.

"The people with the train will be so happy to see the soldiers," Josephine said. "A lot of them have about given up hope."

"Not me," Hortense said. "I never give up."

Fargo went and fetched the Ovaro.

They fell quiet.

It wasn't long before hooves thudded, and Jacob Coarse and Treach and the other two returned leading their mounts.

Fargo saw to it that their rifles were shoved in their saddle scabbards and their sidearms were placed in saddlebags. He didn't mention that he knew about Treach's hideout. He asked the women to douse the fire. As soon as everyone was mounted, he reined to the rear.

"How are you going to lead us from back there?" Jacob Coarse asked.

"We'll follow my tracks."

His trail of disturbed snow was plain enough a child could follow it. Coarse took the lead, his men after him, and then the women.

Fargo came last, his hand always on the Colt.

Not much was said. They'd descended about halfway when Fargo gigged the Ovaro up to Josephine and Hortense. "I have a question."

"You're not my type," Hortense said.

"Will you please be nice?" Josephine said. "I'm sure he doesn't want to go to bed with you."

Fargo wouldn't mind but that wasn't his question. "Have you seen any sign of Blackjack Tar?"

Josephine shook her head. "We know he's out there somewhere. Mr. Coarse has warned us about him time and again."

"Not that I trust Jacob Coarse but it could explain all the people who have disappeared," Hortense said.

"Why didn't others from the train come with you?" Fargo wondered.

"That's two questions," Hortense said.

"We didn't tell anyone we were leaving," Josephine answered. "We were afraid they'd tell Coarse. But he found out anyway."

"The way he's been eyeing us this whole trip," Hortense said, "he must have noticed we were gone soon after we lit a shuck."

"Eyeing you?" Fargo said.

Josephine blushed. "He undresses us with his eyes. It got so, it made my skin itch." She smiled sweetly. "Thank goodness you don't do that. I could tell you were a man of virtue the moment we met."

"That's me," Fargo said. "Virtuous as hell."

19

Fargo stayed at the rear until they were a hundred yards out from the camp. Then he gigged the Ovaro to the front and rose in the stirrups and hailed the soldiers. It puzzled him when they didn't reply. A tap of his spurs brought him out of the last of the trees, and he drew rein in consternation.

A few wisps of smoke curled and a few embers glowed but the fire had almost died out.

Jules, the soldiers and their prisoners, and the horses were gone.

"What the hell?" Fargo blurted. Dismounting, he held on to the reins and sought clues to what had happened. Red spots near the fire caught his eye. He went over and sank to a knee and touched one. It was blood, all right, not quite dry.

Standing, Fargo saw where the snow had been churned by a lot of feet and hooves; the tracks led to the south.

Jules and the troopers had ridden off in a hurry. But why, when they knew he was due back before nightfall? "This makes no damn sense," he said out loud.

"It does to me," Hortense said.

Fargo turned.

The women and Coarse and his men had drawn rein and were staring at him with mixtures of suspicion and hostility.

"Where are the soldiers you told us about?" Josephine asked. "Why aren't they here?"

"I can answer that," Hortense said. "There never were any soldiers. He fed us a lie. He's one of Tar's men, as I've been saying all along. And they rode off and left him."

"The only part that you got right is that they rode off," Fargo said sourly. He was tired of her accusing him.

Jacob Coarse leaned on his saddle horn. "I have my doubts too, mister. I took you at your word and came with you but it's mighty strange these blue coats you're with have up and vanished."

"Just like your people at the wagon train," Fargo said.

Coarse's jaw muscles worked and he glared at the women. "Told him everything, did you?"

"Why shouldn't we?" Josephine said.

"Because if he's one of Tar's men, like Hortense thinks, then he's our enemy."

"He hasn't tried to hurt us," Josephine said.

"He held us at gunpoint," Coarse reminded her. "He made us put up our hardware."

The man with the scar twisted and put his hand on his saddlebags. "I'm getting my pistol out right now."

"Go ahead and try, Treach," Fargo said, placing his hand on his Colt.

"You see?" Coarse said to Josephine. "If he was on our side, would he do something like that?"

"I don't know," Josephine said uncertainly.

"Well, I do," Hortense said, and without warning she slapped her legs against her mare and rode straight at Fargo.

Letting go of the Ovaro's reins, Fargo leaped aside. He was a shade too slow. The mare clipped him and sent him staggering a couple of steps. He regained his balance and saw that Treach had a saddlebag open and was sliding a hand in. "Don't!"

With a snarl of defiance, Treach whipped his revolver out, cocking it as he raised it to shoot.

Fargo drew and fanned a shot from the hip, his hand slapping the hammer hard.

At the blast, Treach was punched half around. The slug had caught him high in the right shoulder. His revolver fell from fingers gone limp and he folded over his saddle horn and groaned.

Fargo covered the others. "Anyone else?"

Jacob Coarse and the other two sat perfectly still. "You miserable bastard," Coarse said.

Josephine cried, "Hortense, no!"

Fargo spun. The redhead was bearing down on him again. This time he sprang out of the way, lunged, and wrapped his left hand around her leg. With a powerful wrench he tore her boot from the stirrup, and heaved.

Hortense yipped as she tumbled to earth in a windmill of limbs. The snow cushioned her fall and she sat up sputtering and wiping at her eyes and nose. "Damn you anyhow!" she fumed.

"Everyone off their horses," Fargo commanded.

"To think I took you at your word," Jacob Coarse snarled as he climbed down.

Josephine, though, didn't. She reined over to Treach, who was still bent over his saddle horn, and gently touched him, saying, "You poor man. Is there anything I can do?"

"Leave him be and get off," Fargo said.

"I will not," Josephine replied. "He's hurt, and I'm a nurse. Helping people is what I do."

Not taking his eyes off the others, Fargo sidled over to Treach's animal. "You heard the lady," he said. "Climb down."

All Treach did was groan louder. Blood dripped from under his sleeve and spattered the snow.

"Give him a hand," Josephine requested.

"Sure," Fargo said. Reaching up, he gripped the back of Treach's coat and pulled.

Treach stirred and clutched at his saddle horn but it was too little, too late. In a spray of snow, he landed with a thud at Fargo's feet.

"That was awful," Josephine said.

"You wanted him off."

Alighting, Josephine dipped to her knees. "Mr. Treach?" She carefully slid her hand under his other shoulder and tried to turn him over. "Can you hear me? You're losing a lot of blood. I need to bandage you."

"If he dies," Jacob Coarse said to Fargo, "you'll answer for it."

Fargo had forgotten about Hortense. He was reminded when Josephine looked past him and again shouted, "Hortense, no!" He started to turn, and a wildcat was on him. The impact nearly knocked him over. He got his arm up but not before she'd raked his cheek and his neck with her fingernails. Cuffing her on the chin, he barked, "That's enough."

"Not hardly," Hortense replied, and threw herself at him anew.

Fargo's patience snapped. He drove his left fist into her gut, doubling her in half, and dropped her with a light rap of the Colt to her temple.

"Hortense!" Josephine cried. Leaving Treach, she darted over and cradled Hortense's head in her lap. "What have you done? If you've hurt her I'll never forgive you."

Fargo wiped the back of his hand across his cheek. It came away streaked with blood. "She damn near took out my eye out."

"That's no excuse."

One of the men with Jacob Coarse took a step toward him, and Fargo covered him. It was the last straw. "Take your rope off your horse," he told the wagon master.

"What for?"

Fargo cocked the Colt.

Muttering, Coarse complied.

"Now get the knife Treach keeps up his sleeve and cut the rope into foot-long lengths."

"You're not fixing to do what I think you're fixing to do?" Coarse said.

"Do it."

Fargo had Jacob Coarse tie the other two and then instructed Josephine to tie Coarse.

"What if I refuse?"

"I'll shoot him."

"Why him and not me?"

"You're prettier."

While Josephine tended to Treach, who had passed out, Fargo rekindled the fire and filled his coffeepot with snow. He put it on to melt, and turned to Hortense and tied her wrists.

"What did you do that for?" Josephine demanded.

Fargo touched the marks on his cheek. "I can't trust any of you."

Jacob Coarse swore. "*You* can't trust *us*? Mister, that would be funny if you were trussed up and not us."

"I can gag you, too," Fargo warned.

Once the water was hot enough, Josephine washed Treach's wound. The slug had gone clean through but nicked a vein.

"So much blood," Josephine said. "You'd better pray he pulls through or you'll have murdered him."

"He was about to murder me," Fargo pointed out.

"You don't know that. It could be he only meant to scare you or wound you."

"And it could be I piss gold after every glass of whiskey," Fargo said. "But I don't."

"You're terribly crude," Josephine said, yet she grinned.

Once she was done bandaging Treach, Fargo added more snow and put coffee on to perk.

"How can you think of that at a time like this?" Josephine asked.

Fargo gave her body a once-over, and smiled. "Did you have something else in mind?"

"Oh my," Josephine said. "I don't understand you. If I came back and found the soldiers I claimed to be with gone, I'd stay in the saddle and go find out where they got to."

"If they're not back by morning, we will."

"Why wait so long? What not head out now?"

Fargo indicated the sun, which was low on the horizon. "We wouldn't get half a mile before we'd have to stop for the night anyway. We might as well stay here."

At that juncture Hortense moaned and rolled onto her side and opened her eyes. She tried to sit up and discovered her arms were bound. "What the hell?"

"It was his doing," Josephine said.

If looks could kill, Hortense's would have dropped Fargo where he sat. "I demand that you release me."

"Did you hear something?" Fargo said to Josephine. "A fly buzzing around?"

"Go to hell," Hortense said.

The sun slowly sank, the shadows spreading and merging until the mountains became cloaked in twilight.

Fargo sat with his tin cup in his hands, the warmth a welcome reprieve. He ignored the glares of Hortense and Jacob Coarse.

Josephine was deep in thought. She had her knees tucked to her chest and her arms wrapped around her legs. "So will you tie me up too before we bed down for the night?"

Fargo grinned. "I had other ideas," he joked.

To his considerable astonishment, Josephine leaned toward him, placed her hands on her thighs, and whispered, "I was hoping you would say that. As soon as the others fall asleep, you can have me."

20

Jacob Coarse was the last to succumb to slumber. Along about ten he closed his eyes and was breathing heavily.

Josephine had pretended to turn in so that, as she put it, "Hortense won't suspect I'm about to be naughty." As soon as Coarse started snoring, she cast off her blanket and sat up and winked at Fargo. "Now it's just you and me," she whispered.

Fargo had something to do first. "I'll be right back." Rising, he moved to the trees and was doing what a lot of coffee gave every man the urge to do when Josephine came up behind him.

"We have to find somewhere they can't see us in case one of them wakes up."

"It will be hard to find a dry spot in all this snow," Fargo mentioned.

"I'm sure you'll think of something."

"You're awful cheerful," Fargo remarked as he stuffed himself into his pants.

"Why wouldn't I be? You coming along has been a godsend."

"Treach wouldn't think so."

"He shouldn't have tried to draw on you."

"Hortense would—" Fargo began, and got no farther. She stepped up close, wrapped her arms around his waist, and pressed her cheek to his bearskin coat.

"You smell like bear," she said.

"Wonder why."

"This isn't something I would ordinarily do."

"Make love?"

"No," Josephine said, stepping back.

Fargo felt her hands move and looked down. His holster was empty. "Damn."

Josephine pointed his Colt and cocked it. "Please don't try anything. I'd rather not shoot you if I can help it."

"It was a trick," Fargo said, furious at himself over how gullible he'd been.

"I'm sorry. But mark my words. I will shoot if you force me."

The mix of firelight and shadow gave her face a steely cast.

"I don't doubt it," Fargo said.

"It's Hortense. I can't bear to see her treated like that. You have to set her free. And while you're at it, set Mr. Coarse and the others free, as well."

"I thought you didn't trust him."

"I don't. But better the devil you know than one you've just met."

"And if you're wrong?"

"I'll have to live with the consequences." Josephine motioned. "Come on. Slowly, if you please. I wouldn't want to squeeze this trigger by mistake."

"I wouldn't want you to, either."

The rest were fast asleep, Coarse snoring loud enough to shake buildings.

"Hortense first," Josephine said. "And please don't try anything. For your own good."

"I wouldn't think of it," Fargo said. When in truth he had been thinking of nothing but and waiting for the perfect chance. She gave it to him by coming closer as he bent over Hortense. With a swiftness that startled her, he whirled, grabbed the Colt and slipped his thumb under the hammer to prevent her from firing, and wrenched the six-gun from her hand.

"Oh! How did you do that?"

"Quickly," Fargo said.

"What now? Will you shoot me?"

"And here I'd pegged you as the one with brains," Fargo said wearily. He made her lie down, tied her wrists, and pulled her blanket up to keep her warm.

"I don't suppose if I gave you my word I'd behave that you'd set me free?"

"I try not to make the same mistake twice." Reclaiming his seat, Fargo finished the last of the coffee.

The night was as quiet as before. Not a single howl or hoot disturbed the abyss.

By the North Star it was pushing one when he added wood to the fire, curled on his side, and let himself drift off. He needed rest. It promised to be a long day tomorrow.

Cold woke him. The fire had almost gone out and dawn wasn't far off.

Sitting up, Fargo stretched and shivered and set about his morning ritual of stoking the embers and putting more coffee on. He sometimes wondered which he drank more of, coffee or whiskey. He figured it was coffee but not by much.

The crackling and the aroma woke the others.

Hortense and Jacob Coarse took up where they'd left off, and glared.

Treach groaned and asked for water and Fargo gave him some.

"That was nice of you," Josephine said. "Maybe I was wrong. An outlaw wouldn't be so considerate."

"Buttering me up won't work a second time," Fargo said.

"How about some food?" Jacob Coarse demanded. "Or do you aim to starve us?"

"There's a notion," Fargo said.

"What *are* your plans?" Josephine asked.

"To head out and find the soldiers."

"Not them again," Hortense said. "Can't you come up with any new lies?"

That was when a horse whinnied off in the forest and the clatter of accoutrements heralded the arrival of Jules and Sergeant Petrie and the troopers under him. They looked as if they had been through hell.

Private Benton's left arm was in a sling with a large bloodstain.

Jules drew rein, pushed his hat back on his head, and regarded the figures sprawled around the fire. "Starting a collection of your own?"

Hortense's eyes were saucers of white. "There really *are* soldiers!" she exclaimed.

"Tired ones," Sergeant Petrie said. He dismounted and accepted a cup of coffee from Fargo. "We both have some explaining to do. How about I go first?"

"Fletcher and Margaret got away," Fargo guessed.

Petrie nodded. "He had a knife hid on him somewhere and cut his bonds. Benton was standing guard while the rest of us were in the trees trying to find firewood. Fletcher stabbed him and knocked him down with his own rifle, and freed the woman. We chased them most of the day and lost their trail when they took to a stream. So we turned around and came back."

"Hold on," Fargo said, and looked around. "Where's Captain Griffin?"

"You didn't see it?" Jules asked.

"See what?"

Jules reined over to a long white hump where the trees met the clearing. "We buried him shallow and covered the body with snow. It was the best we could do with the ground froze."

"The captain had stayed in camp," Sergeant Petrie

said. "He must have tried to stop Fletcher and the woman and one or the other stabbed him in the heart."

"Want to bet they find her brother and join up with him?" Jules speculated.

"If anyone knows where Tar is hiding out, it's her," Petrie agreed, and turned to Fargo. "Your turn."

It didn't take long for Fargo to relate all that had happened since he had left the day before.

"We've both been busy," Petrie said wearily. He proceeded to give orders. While two troopers saw to their horses, two others untied the women and the wagon master and his men.

Jacob Coarse seemed dazed. He stared at the soldiers as if he couldn't quite believe they were real.

"Don't you worry, Mr. Coarse," Sergeant Petrie assured him. "We'll see your people safely down these mountains and all the way to Fort Laramie."

Coarse had been strangely quiet but he found his voice to say, "We're headed in the other direction."

"I know. You're bound for Oregon. But your people will need to rest up after their ordeal. The fort is the safest place around."

"I'll have to think it over."

"You don't have a say," Petrie informed him. "I'm under orders to take you and your wagons down, and that's exactly what I'm going to do."

"It's high-handed of the army," Coarse complained.

"Not when it's in your own best interests."

Since the troopers had ridden half the night, they were permitted to sleep until noon. Jules turned in, as well.

Coarse wanted to head back to his train but Petrie told him they'd all go together.

Fargo was left pretty much on his own and liked it that way. He roosted on a log and was nibbling on pemmican when Josephine and Hortense walked over. "Go away," he said.

"We're sorry," Josephine said.

"Go away anyway."

"We were wrong about you," Josephine said, "and we apologize."

"Do you, now."

"You don't have to be so prickly about it," Hortense said. "Don't you ever make mistakes?"

"I try to limit myself to one a day."

"Hardy-har-har," Hortense said. "We're sincere. It wouldn't hurt you to be more understanding and gracious about it."

"Gracious?" Fargo laughed. "You have me confused with someone else."

Hortense harrumphed, wheeled, and stalked away.

"Did you have to do that?" Josephine asked.

"She tried to ride me down."

"She's always been impetuous."

"She tried to claw out my eyes."

"You have to admit she doesn't do things by half."

Despite himself, Fargo laughed.

"We should put all that's happened behind us," Josephine proposed. "Forgive and forget."

"I never forget," Fargo said. "But I'll try if she does."

The sky had cleared and the bright sunshine made the snow hard to look at. The temperature climbed, too, and by midday some of the snow was melting.

By one o'clock the soldiers were up and everyone was in the saddle and headed for the high country meadow where the wagons were stranded.

Josephine gigged her horse next to the Ovaro and breathed in the rarefied air. "It's a beautiful day, isn't it? Wait until everyone sees the soldiers. They'll be giddy that their nightmare is finally and truly over."

"Let's hope," Fargo said.

21

It took three days.

Awash in the bright light of the afternoon sun, the valley was a quarter mile wide and barely that long. A series of gradual slopes led up to it, which explained how the heavy wagons were able to climb so high. But once there they had nowhere to go. The west end was blocked by the thickly timbered slope of a towering mountain.

In the distance, Fargo saw the wagons arranged in a giant circle. Or the tops of them, anyway. They were buried up to their beds in snow.

"Some leader you are," Jules Vallee remarked as they sat their winded horses after climbing the last slope.

"Watch what you say, old man," Jacob Coarse said. "How was I to know this valley was a dead end?"

"You never should have brought those pilgrims up here," Jules said.

"I told you to have a care," Coarse said, and placed his hand on his revolver.

Fargo hadn't wanted to return their weapons, not after Treach pulled on him. But Sergeant Petrie insisted. Now he dropped his own hand to his Colt and said, "You should think twice."

Coarse jerked his hand off his six-shooter. "And you should tell this old buzzard to stop insulting me."

"Time's a-wasting," Josephine declared. "We have to

give everyone the good news." She gigged her horse and Hortense did likewise with her mare.

Coarse motioned at his men and they rode on ahead, too.

Fargo followed at a walk. Jules and the troopers were in no hurry, either.

"I'll be glad when this is over," Sergeant Petrie said. "That wagon master rubs me wrong."

"I get the feeling he's mad at me," Jules responded. "And not just over what I just said."

"You reported Coarse to the army," Fargo reminded him. "You're the reason we're here."

"Why would us coming to save his hash make him mad?" Jules wondered.

"Could be he's upset at having his nose rubbed in how stupid he's been," Sergeant Petrie said.

Fargo squinted against the glare, seeking sign of people moving about, and campfire smoke. "That's strange."

"What is, pard?" Jules asked.

"Where is everybody?"

Jules shielded his eyes and Petrie stared and the latter said, "Damned odd. I don't see a living soul."

Josephine and Hortense reached the train first and commenced to shout, calling out names.

Sergeant Petrie jabbed his spurs. "If anything has happened to these people—"

Canvas rustled in the wind but not a solitary head poked out as they approached. The inside of the circle had been cleared of snow. Two large cooking pots hung on bipods over the charcoal remnants of fires.

Josephine and Hortense had climbed down and were running from wagon to wagon.

"No one!" Josephine cried as she peered into another. "They're all gone."

"They were here when we left," Hortense said, equally anxious.

Petrie instructed his men to conduct a thorough sweep, and joined them.

Fargo noticed that Jacob Coarse hadn't dismounted and seemed the least agitated by the absence of those he'd been hired to guide. "Don't you care that everyone is gone?"

"Of course I do," Coarse said grumpily. "Mind your own business. Come on, boys." He led his men toward the far side of the circle.

Jules said, "You know what this means, don't you, pard?"

"About Coarse?"

"About Blackjack Tar. He must have caught the pilgrims with their britches down."

"Where are the bodies?"

Jules had no answer to that. Nor did anyone else. Every wagon was searched, every square inch of ground. The wagons were undamaged, the possessions piled inside intact.

It was a bewildered group that gathered in the center.

"Don't this beat all?" Jules said. "All these folks, up and disappearing."

"We told you," Josephine said. "People have been vanishing all along."

"Maybe they wandered off and got lost," Jacob Coarse suggested.

"All of them at the same time?" Sergeant Petrie said. "Don't spout nonsense."

"Their teams are gone too," Fargo mentioned.

Everyone else glanced around as if realizing it for the first time.

"I'll be damned," Jules said.

"Maybe it was hostiles." Jacob Coarse offered another reason. "The Blackfeet like to steal horses almost as much as they like to kill whites."

"We haven't come across a lick of Injun sign," Jules said.

By now, Fargo reckoned, the Ovaro had rested enough. He stepped to the stallion, swung up, and announced, "I might be gone a day or two."

"Where the hell are you off to?" Jacob Coarse asked gruffly.

"Where the hell do you think?"

"Hold on," Petrie said. "I'll send a couple of my men along."

"It's better if it's just me." To forestall a debate, Fargo left the circle. Since the west end of the valley was blocked and they had entered it from the east and not seen signs of a mass exodus, that left north and south. He looped south.

He figured to find a wide swath of trampled snow. Instead, he found a narrow line of tracks where the people from the train had walked in single file. Or, rather, been forced to walk.

On both sides of the line were the hoofprints of their captors.

It boggled the brain.

Based on what Josephine and Hortense had told him, there were close to three dozen emigrants left, three dozen men, women, and children who were now in the clutches of the terror of the territory. Blackjack Tar could do with them as he pleased, and by all accounts, what pleased him most was torture and killing.

Where Tar could be taking them, Fargo had no idea.

The tracks were two to three days old.

Fargo half expected the trail would take him deep into the mountains but he hadn't been at it an hour when he spied gray spirals.

The proximity to the canyon where the wagon train became stranded fueled a suspicion he'd been harboring.

Fargo slowed.

The smoke rose from a slight escarpment that overlooked the surrounding countryside. If not for the snow, tracking them would have been considerably harder. The ground was bedrock, or mostly so.

The escarpment was crisscrossed with bluffs, creating a virtual maze. The outlaws had made the pilgrims slog along a winding path with more twists and turns than a slithering snake.

When he smelled smoke, Fargo shucked the Henry from the saddle scabbard and levered a round into the chamber. There were bound to be lookouts, he reasoned. He scanned the bluffs on either side but saw no one.

A whinny brought him to a stop. He strained his ears and heard voices, too.

At the base of a bluff to his left were several boulders the size of outhouses. He reined in among them. They didn't hide the stallion completely but it was the best he could do.

From there he advanced on foot. He wasn't worried about the tracks he left; they were only a few among scores.

Staying close to the bluff, Fargo came to a bend. He took off his hat and peered around.

He was boggled a second time.

A broad open area was hemmed by other bluffs, creating a sort of natural bowl. A ribbon of a stream had been dammed to make a pond that had partly frozen over. A long lean-to constructed from pine boughs served as a stable. Two cabins, crude but stout, told Fargo that this was what lawmen and the army would give anything to find: Blackjack Tar's hideout.

The bluff walls were unusual. They were pockmarked with hollows that lent them the look of beehives. At first glance Fargo thought they were caves. Then he saw that the holes didn't go in more than a dozen feet. And in many of them figures were sprawled, bound hand and foot.

He had found the emigrants. The children were conspicuous by their small size.

Fargo's jaw muscles clenched. He had a reputation for being as hard as nails. Maybe he was. But there were certain lines he didn't cross and doing harm to kids was one of them.

The outlaws were so confident they were safe in their sanctuary, they'd built not one, not two, but three fires. It made more sense for them to be in the cabins where they'd be snug and warm, only then they couldn't keep an eye on their captives.

Fargo counted twelve. He'd heard enough about Blackjack Tar to know that none of those at the fires fit Tar's description.

Then a cabin door opened and out strode a man who did. Blackjack Tar was a two-legged bear. Everything about him was bearish, from his enormous bulk and his bristly hair and beard to the hell-lit eyes that blazed from a face so bearlike, the resemblance was uncanny. The bearskin coat he wore heightened the effect, especially since it hadn't been fashioned from a black bear hide, like Fargo's, but from a grizzly's. A brace of pistols was strapped around his waist as was a pair of knives, and the hilt of a third knife stuck from the top of a boot.

Tar moved like a bear, too, with a ponderous gait that was deceptive. Fargo had heard the man was quick on his feet.

Two people came out of the cabin after him: Margaret and Fletcher.

"Well, now," Fargo said under his breath.

Blackjack Tar walked to a fire and held his big hands out to warm them. He stared at the hollows in the bluffs and said in a voice that boomed twice as loud as most, "I reckon it's getting on to time, boys."

"Starting in a little early today, ain't you?" asked a man who wore a mackinaw.

"We got so many," Blackjack Tar said.

"Hell, we got 'em to spare," declared another outlaw, and laughed.

Margaret was bundled in a coat, her hands in the pockets. "Do I get to join in the fun?"

"When do I ever tell you no, sis?" Blackjack Tar replied. He bent and drew the knife from his boot and held it so it caught the sun and the blade gleamed. "I think I'll start with a female, boys. Go fetch me one."

22

Two of the outlaws rose and hurried toward a bluff. They entered a hollow and a commotion ensued. There was the sound of a blow. The next moment the outlaws reappeared, dragging a woman.

Fargo drew back and jammed his hat on. He should have listened to Sergeant Petrie and brought a few troopers along.

The outlaws at the other fires didn't seem particularly interested in what was going on. Maybe they'd seen their infamous leader torture so many people, it wasn't anything special.

Blackjack Tar grinned and thwacked his thumbnail against the knife blade, making it ring. "What do we have here?"

The two outlaws dumped the woman at his feet and stepped back.

"She's a pretty one," Margaret said.

The woman wasn't much over twenty, with copper hair and green eyes filled with terror. Her homespun dress had been torn and she had a bruise on her cheek. "What do you want?" she anxiously asked. "Why are you doing this? What did we ever do to you?"

"Questions, questions," Blackjack Tar said. "They always have questions."

His men laughed.

Tar squatted and held the tip of his knife to the woman's nose. "How about I cut this off to start."

"Please," the woman pleaded, tears beginning to stream. "Don't hurt me."

"Why in hell do you think I brought you here?" Blackjack Tar said. He gestured at the bluffs with their beehives. "Why I brought all of you?"

"Not just for the purpose of killing us? That would be inhuman."

"You stupid cow. I can't steal all your wagons and possessions with you still in them, now, can I?" Blackjack Tar said, to more laughter.

"But . . . but . . ." the woman sputtered. "There are so many of us."

"The more, the bloodier."

"We have children."

"Young or old, what's the difference?" Tar rejoined. "Dead is dead."

"Oh God," the woman gasped.

Blackjack Tar gazed at the sky and spread his huge arms. "You hear her up there? She's calling on you for help. If you're going to strike me down, you'd better get to it."

His men thought he was hilarious. Fletcher joined in their mirth, and Margaret said in delight, "You're always such a hoot, brother."

Blackjack waited, and when a lightning bolt out of the blue didn't sear him, he looked down at the woman. "I reckon the Almighty thinks you're not worth saving."

"Please," she said.

"Blubber all you want," Tar said. "I like it when they blubber."

"What manner of man are you?"

Blackjack put his other hand to his chin and rubbed his beard. "A hairy one."

The woman bowed her head and let out a sob. "How can you joke about something like this?"

"Like what?" Blackjack said. "I ain't even started yet."

"You're fixing to kill me."

"Not for a while. I like to take my time."

The woman looked up. "How about," she said, and nervously licked her lips, "how about I give you something better?"

"What would that be?"

"Me," the woman said, and swallowed. "Don't hurt me and you can have me."

"I have you anyhow," Blackjack said, and some of his men snickered and smirked.

"No, I mean you can *have* me."

"Speak plain," Blackjack taunted.

"I'll let you make love to me if you don't kill me," the woman offered.

Blackjack threw back his head and cackled, then abruptly sobered. "I can poke you any damn time I want. But that's not half as much fun as the other."

"The other?"

Blackjack jabbed her arm lightly with the tip of his knife. "The blood and the screams."

"God Almighty."

"Not Him again." Blackjack reached out and tore a button from her dress. "I reckon we should get to it."

The woman recoiled and said, "My husband will get you for this."

About to reach for another button, Blackjack said, "Your husband? Where's he?"

"In the same hole you threw me in."

Blackjack looked at one of the two outlaws he'd had bring her. "Buck, you know which one is her man?"

Buck nodded. "He tried to stop us and I pistol-whipped the bastard."

"Shoot him."

"No!" the woman cried. "I beg you! Don't kill him because of me!"

"I'm going to kill all of you sooner or later. Now is as good as any other."

The woman began to bawl.

Margaret scrunched up her face in disgust. "This one's pathetic. Slit her throat and be done with it."

"Now, now, sis," Blackjack said. "I don't like to rush."

Fargo had a decision to make. He could go back for Petrie and the soldiers, but by the time they returned the woman would be long dead. Or he could go up against the worst pack of killers this side of anywhere by his lonesome.

Wedging the Henry to his shoulder, he took a bead on Blackjack Tar. Shooting the bastard would bring the rest down on him in a mad rush, and he'd be as good as dead.

He had to do this smart.

Tar had pushed the woman flat and was prying at her dress. She whimpered and squirmed.

Thumbing the hammer back, Fargo held his breath to steady his aim, and stroked the trigger.

At the blast several things happened. Blackjack Tar's hat arced into the air and flipped end over end. The outlaws all leaped to their feet, turned and saw the Henry, and froze.

"The next one is in your head, Tar," Fargo hollered. "Unless you do as I say."

"Fargo!" Margaret cried.

"Who?" Blackjack said. Like the others he had turned to stone but he showed no alarm or fear. If anything, he was too calm.

"Skye Fargo," Margaret said. "The one I told you about, remember?"

"The famous scout," Blackjack Tar said. He smiled and raised his already loud voice. "I owe you, mister. You put a stop to my operation at the trading post."

"That was your doing?" Fargo said while watching the

rest. The outlaws were looking at Tar, taking their cue from him.

"It's all my doing," Blackjack boasted.

"The wagon train, too," Fargo said. It was too much of a coincidence, the wagons becoming stranded so close to Tar's hole in the wall.

"Aren't you the clever pup," Blackjack said, and laughed. "How do you aim to play this, mister?"

"Drop the knife and come toward me with your hands in the air."

"And if I don't?"

Fargo shot Fletcher in the head.

Margaret screamed. Some of the outlaws swore. Fletcher took a tottering step and oozed into a lifeless pile with scarlet dribbling from the bullet hole.

"That answer your question?" Fargo shouted.

"Sure does," Blackjack replied. He was grinning.

Margaret stared at the body of her lover. With an inarticulate cry, she opened her coat and swooped her hand to a revolver on her hip.

"No!" Blackjack commanded.

Margaret stopped and looked at him.

"He'll kill you," Blackjack said.

Hate turned Margaret ugly. But she jerked her hand off her six-shooter. "Fine. But when the time comes, he's mine—you hear?"

"Finders keepers," Blackjack said. Dropping the knife, he stood and raised his arms over his head. "How's this?"

"Come ahead," Fargo said. "Your men try to shoot me, you're the first to join Fletcher in hell."

"You heard him," Blackjack said to the others. "Not a finger—you hear?"

"But, boss—" Buck said.

"He won't shoot me as long as you stay close," Blackjack said, and grinned, "so stay close." Swaggering toward Fargo, he smiled, treating the whole thing as a great game.

"Having fun?" Fargo asked when the human bear was closer.

"You've done me a great favor," Blackjack Tar said.

"I must have missed it."

"Fletcher. I never much liked him. I didn't think he was good enough for my sis. But I couldn't shoot him myself or she wouldn't speak to me."

"You're welcome," Fargo said.

Blackjack Tar stopped and looked him up and down. "Nice coat. Griz is warmer, though."

"Here's what I want," Fargo said. "Have your men untie the emigrants."

"No," Blackjack said.

"They don't, I'll shoot you. I'm taking those people to their wagons and taking you as insurance your men won't try anything."

"No and no."

"You're not listening." Fargo put his cheek to the Henry and fixed a bead on Tar's broad face. "We do this my way or else."

"Or else what?" Blackjack said. "You'll kill me?" He chuckled. "Go ahead. My men will be on you before you can spit, and that will be that." He shook his head. "No. What we have here is a standoff."

Fargo was tempted to say to hell with it and stroke the trigger anyway. Then an idea occurred to him. "Who said it has to be you?"

"Who else?"

"That bitch of a sister of yours."

"The hell you say."

Fargo shifted and aimed at Margaret. "Care to bet I won't?"

"A man after my own heart," Blackjack Tar said, and did the last thing Fargo imagined—Tar laughed. "Go ahead and splatter her brains."

23

Fargo raised his cheek from the Henry.

"Surprised?" Blackjack Tar asked. "A brother shouldn't want his own sis to feed the worms? But you just said it yourself. She's the biggest bitch this side of the Mississippi."

"I can't believe you don't give a damn about your own sister," Fargo admitted.

Blackjack Tar folded those huge arms of his. "That's how it always is. Folks can't believe I like to cut people into pieces, but I do. They can't believe I'll roast a man over a spit, but I have. They can't believe I'll stake out kids for the ants to feed on, but I've done that more times than you can count."

Fargo almost shot him then and there.

"People think that everyone thinks the same as they do," Blackjack rumbled on. "I doubt there's ten men on this continent who think like me."

"Brag a lot?"

"You know it's true," Blackjack said. "If you ask me, I should have been born an Apache. I hear they like to carve on folks as much as I do."

"They do it to test their enemy's courage. You do it for the thrill."

"A man should like his work."

"Is that what you call it?"

"Friend . . ." Blackjack began.

"That's one thing we'll never be," Fargo broke in.

"Friend," Blackjack said again. "Your problem is that you don't do what you have to when you have to. If you had a lick of brains, you'd have shot me by now."

"I have other plans."

"To turn me over to the cavalry? My sister told me there were only six blue coats with you. Do you honestly think that's enough?"

"For most it would be."

Blackjack Tar shook his head. "We both know how this will end. Take my advice and light a shuck while you can."

"I've never been fond of tucking tail," Fargo said. "It puts a crease in my ass."

Blackjack Tar loved that one. When he was done laughing he said, "Time to make up your mind. Skedaddle or face a dozen killers who'd think no more of burying you than they would of squashing a bug."

"You speak for all of them?"

"Always have, always will," Blackjack said. "They do exactly as I say and never give me sass. Except Margaret, the bitch of bitches."

Fargo noticed that true to Tar's boast, not one outlaw had moved from where they stood.

"Another reason you should tuck tail," Tar said, "is that all I have to do is give a holler and they'll be on you like wolves on a lame elk."

"I'm not lame," Fargo said, and once again he aimed at the killer in the grizzly coat. "And this is my last warning."

Blackjack lowered his arms. "I reckon you have to do it, then." He raised his voice. "Buck? Margaret? If you hear a shot, kill this bastard."

"You can count on us," Buck hollered.

"There you go," Blackjack said with a smile.

Fargo had bluffed and lost. It was just his luck to run into someone who never, ever backed down.

"Aim good," Blackjack said. "I want it quick and pain-less."

Fargo had a thought. "Painless, hell," he said. "I'll shoot you in the knee first. Ever had your knee broke?" When Tar shook his head he said, "People say it's the worst pain a man can feel next to kidney stones. You won't be able to stand, and while you're thrashing around and cussing me, I'll shoot you in the balls."

"You're a damn bastard."

"Two or three shots," Fargo said. "Enough to mangle your nuts and maybe shoot off your pecker."

"You're a miserable damn bastard." Blackjack looked down at himself and scowled. "That's plumb mean."

"Listen to the pot call the kettle black."

Blackjack looked up and went to say something. His gaze drifted past Fargo and he gave a slight start and smiled. "What do we have here? Appears to me you're about to be caught between a rock and a hard place."

"That trick is as old as the hills," Fargo said. Then a hoof thudded, and he took a step back and glanced over his shoulder, and swore.

Sergeant Petrie and Private Benton and another trooper were coming up the canyon. All three were bound. The third trooper had been shot in the shoulder and it was still bleeding.

Behind them were Jacob Coarse and two of Coarse's men, with their pistols leveled. Coarse drew rein and snapped something at the others and they stopped. "Black-jack?" he yelled. "What in hell is going on?"

"The scout has me at his mercy," Tar answered in great amusement.

"Drop that rifle, mister," Jacob Coarse bellowed, "or we shoot the soldiers."

"I'd listen to him," Blackjack said. "He likes to kill almost as much as I do."

Fargo had a question to ask first. "Was it your notion

or his to bring that wagon train up here and strand them?"

"Another of my many brainstorms," Blackjack said. "Why go hunting for folks to rob and kill when we can trick them into coming to us? I had Coarse go to Missouri and hire himself out as a wagon boss. He'd done it a few times years ago, before he turned to stealing for a living."

"I have to hand it to you," Fargo said. "That's as clever as they come."

Blackjack was pleased by the flattery. "I haven't lasted as long as I have by being stupid." He paused and held out his hand. "Now, then. Do you hand me that rifle or does Coarse put holes in those troopers?"

It went against Fargo's grain. His natural instinct was to fight. To spill as much of their blood as he could before they spilled his. Instead, he frowned and let down the Henry's hammer and gave the rifle to Tar.

Blackjack beamed. "It's not often some gent gets the drop on me. You had me worried for a bit. You truly did." He held out his other hand. "Your six-shooter, if you don't mind, and even if you do."

Fargo gave the Colt to him.

Blackjack stepped back and motioned at Jacob Coarse. "Bring them on," he commanded. He then motioned for Fargo to walk ahead of him, saying, "I believe I'll let you live a while. I have to come up with something special for a gent like you."

"Go to hell."

"No, you've been right reasonable about this," Blackjack said. "And you're not scared of me. That there is reason enough for me to like you."

"I must have missed something," Fargo said.

"What you've missed is being me. It's always there. In their eyes. The fear. I like it when I'm carving on folks. I don't like it from my own men."

"Why the hell are you telling me this?"

145

"I don't rightly know," Tar said, and started to laugh but cut it short. "Here now. What's this?"

Margaret had a pistol in her hand and was marching toward them with storm clouds on her brow. Her eyes were narrowed and her nostrils flared and she was red with fury.

Buck and several other outlaws were hurrying to catch up.

Blackjack stepped in front of Fargo and stopped. "What's with the smoke wagon, sis?"

"Out of my way," Margaret snarled, gesturing. "He killed Fletch and I will by God do the same to him."

"Not until and unless I say you can," Blackjack told her.

"Out of my way, damn it." Margaret raised her revolver. Her eyes brimmed with tears. "You know how much Fletcher meant to me."

"When I tell someone to do something," Blackjack said, "they damn well better do it. Even you."

"I'm your sister!" Margaret practically yelled.

"Which is why I won't skin you alive." Tar nodded at Buck, who had come up behind her.

Before Margaret realized what was happening, the outlaws were on her. They seized her arms and Buck grabbed her six-gun. It went off, the slug digging a furrow in the snow at Blackjack's feet. Buck wrested it from her grasp and she clawed at his face.

"Hold her, damn it," Buck said.

Blackjack stepped past him. He had tucked Fargo's Colt under his belt and his big hand rose and fell. He didn't use his fist. His open palm was enough. There was a slap and Margaret went limp. It was an incredible display of strength; Fargo knew firsthand how tough Margaret was.

"I didn't want to do that," Blackjack said.

"What do we do with her?" Buck asked. "Tie her and throw her in one of the holes?"

"My own sister?" Blackjack said.

"You were willing to let the scout shoot her," Buck said. "We heard you."

"So you got it into that little head of yours that I don't care for her?"

Something in Blackjack's tone made Buck blanch and take a step back. "I don't know what to think."

Blackjack placed a hand on one of his bowies.

"I let you do my thinking for me."

Grinning, Blackjack removed his hand from the hilt. "You've just saved your life." He gave Buck a pat on the arm. "Take my sister to my cabin. When she comes to give her some whiskey. I'll be along in a bit."

"And if she tries to leave?"

"Don't let her. Don't hurt her, but don't let her."

"It'll be like trying to hold a wildcat."

The rest of the outlaws converged. Pistols were drawn and trained on Fargo and everyone moved toward the encampment.

Coarse came up and rode next to Blackjack and the pair talked in low tones.

Fargo glanced at Sergeant Petrie. "They jumped you when your backs were turned?" he guessed.

Petrie glumly nodded. "I never suspected a thing."

Fargo felt a spike of regret for not informing the sergeant of his suspicions.

"Shot my other men where they stood and took the rest of us prisoner."

"Jules and the women?"

Petrie shook his head. "I don't know."

"They weren't with you?"

"They'd gone into the woods for firewood. After Coarse tied us, him and the others went in after them. I heard shouts and shots. When Coarse came back I asked him where the trapper and the ladies were, and he said they're good and dead. His exact words."

"Damn," Fargo said.

24

The screams seared the ear. Broken by intermittent blubbering and cries no human throat should make, they seemed to go on forever.

The begging was the worst. She pleaded. She sobbed. She wailed. She called on God, too, and whenever she did, Blackjack Tar roared with laughter.

Fargo wished he could plug his ears. He was sick of hearing it. Sick, and filled with a simmering rage that filled his veins with fire.

He lay on his side, tied wrists and ankles, in what he had taken to be a second cabin but was in fact something else—a storeroom.

The cabin was crammed with plunder: food, tools, jewelry, guns, ammunition, clothes, clocks, and more. All taken from those the gang had robbed and killed. The wagon train promised to be their richest haul yet.

Sergeant Petrie, Private Benton, and the wounded trooper lay nearby.

Petrie looked at the burlap that covered the window, his face a well of pity. "How much more can he do to that poor woman?"

A high shriek rose to the surrounding peaks.

"What worries me," Private Benton said, his face slick with the sweat of raw fear, "is what he'll do to us."

"Steady, trooper," Sergeant Petrie cautioned. "Don't lose your head. Remember your training."

"We never trained for something like this," Benton said.

The third soldier groaned. "Sarge, I don't feel so good," he said weakly.

"You've lost too much blood," Petrie said. "I don't understand how you could lose so much. You should have stopped bleeding hours ago."

A scarlet pool had formed under the man and was spreading toward the rest of them.

"My ma used to warn me not to get cut when I was little," the man said, his voice so low they barely heard him. "She said our family are bleeders."

"And you enlisted in the army?"

"I always wanted to be a soldier. I wasn't about to let that stop—" He let out a gasp.

"Samuels?" Sergeant Petrie said, and struggled to sit up.

Fargo twisted his head around.

The wounded trooper had gone limp and his tongue lolled from a mouth gone slack. His eyes had rolled up into his head.

"He's gone."

Sergeant Petrie swore. "That makes four I've lost. Benton, do me a favor and try to stay alive."

"I'll try, Sarge," Benton said. "But Blackjack Tar has other ideas."

"If only we could get free," Petrie said, straining mightily.

Fargo had been working at his bonds, prying at the knots to the rope around his ankles to loosen them enough to reach his Arkansas toothpick. So far they had resisted his efforts.

Just then the door opened, admitting a gust of cold air. In walked Jacob Coarse. He smirked and hooked his thumb in his belt. "Tar sent me to check on you," he said. "He has big plans for you."

"Go to hell, you mangy cur," Private Benton said. "You killed my friends."

Coarse turned and kicked him in the stomach, and

when Benton writhed and grimaced, he laughed. "Anything else you want to say?"

Fargo shifted toward him. "Jules Vallee and Josephine and Hortense?"

"What about them?"

"Petrie tells me they're dead?"

Coarse nodded. "They saw us tying these three and ran. We went after them. Must have chased them half a mile up that mountain, swapping lead now and then. The snow got them."

"The snow?"

"An avalanche. I saw it with my own eyes. The snow swept down and buried them alive."

"What a horrible way to die," Sergeant Petrie said.

"Compared to how Tar aims to do you in," Coarse said, "their deaths were downright pleasant." He chortled and strutted out.

"I hate that man," Petrie said. "I want to strangle him with my two hands."

Fargo renewed his assault on the knots but he wasn't getting anywhere. He scanned the stolen goods again. Several knives had been placed on a shelf at the back of the room but getting to them was impossible. He craned his neck farther, and hope flared.

Over in a corner was a mound of clothes. Coats, hats, pants, shirts, everything. Above the mound, hanging from a peg, was a lantern.

With a grunt, Fargo heaved toward the corner. He rolled, and rolled again, wincing as his elbow scraped the plank floor. When he reached the mound he paused and girded himself.

"What are you doing?" Sergeant Petrie asked.

"You want to be free, don't you?" Fargo rejoined, and flung himself up the pile, rolling as fast as he could roll. He got about halfway and the clothes buckled under his weight and he tumbled to the bottom.

"What good is that?" Private Benton asked.

Fargo didn't waste breath explaining. He rolled up the mound, whipping his body as fast as he could. He was almost to the top when once again gravity took over and he rolled back to the floor. "Damn it."

"I see what you're up to," Petrie said. "Want me to try?"

Tensing every muscle, Fargo tried a third time. His previous attempts had flattened part of the mound, making it easier. He reached the top and looked up.

The lantern was still more than two feet over his head.

Swiveling onto his back, Fargo drew his legs to his chest. He experimented with moving the toes of his boots as far apart as he could, which was only a couple of inches and not wide enough to grip the lantern. That left the handle.

Arching his entire body, Fargo carefully straightened his legs as high as they would go. He couldn't quite reach. It didn't help that the clothes under him compressed with his weight and he sank a little lower.

"Keep at it," Sergeant Petrie urged.

As if Fargo wouldn't. His life, their lives, the lives of the emigrants, were at stake. He wouldn't give up this side of the grave.

Gritting his teeth, Fargo raised the tips of his boots higher than the lantern but not high enough, unfortunately, to hook the handle. He bent practically into a bow but had to sink down in defeat, his shoulders and neck throbbing.

"You were so close," Petrie said.

"Don't remind me," Fargo growled. He wriggled to position himself better and this time propped his legs against the wall to spare his shoulders. Then he slowly inched his boots higher until they were even with the lantern. With a flip of his foot, he thrust his boot up and under and hooked the handle. But when he tried to pull the lantern off the peg, the handle snagged. He tried to raise the handle higher but couldn't. Once again he had to lower his legs in defeat.

"I bet I could do it," Private Benton said. "Let me up there."

"You're not as tall as he is," Sergeant Petrie said. "You couldn't raise your legs high enough."

Fargo did more wriggling. When he gauged his position was just right, he speared his boots at the handle, snagged it, and slid it over the peg.

Private Benton whooped for joy.

"Quiet, damn it," Sergeant Petrie said. "They'll hear you."

Fargo tucked his knees to lower the lantern to the pile but it slid off his toes and fell toward his face. He wrenched aside, felt it clip his shoulder, and heard it clatter down the pile. He rolled after it.

The lantern came to rest on the floor.

So did Fargo. Prone on his back, he elevated both legs, made sure his boots were directly over the lantern, and brought them crashing down.

The glass shattered, sending shards every which way.

Some of the pieces were inches long and as wide as Fargo's hand. Turning, he looked over his shoulder and gripped a piece with a sharp edge. He carefully pressed it to the rope and commenced to saw back and forth.

Sergeant Petrie wriggled closer and imitated him. He wasn't as careful and cut his finger.

"Let me in there," Private Benton said. "I want a piece of glass too."

Petrie shook his head. "Roll over to the door and listen. If you hear someone coming, put your back to the door and delay them as long as you can."

"They'll push right on in," Benton said, but he did as he'd been ordered.

Fargo had to press hard to make headway. He felt some strands part, felt the rope give slightly, but it wasn't enough. He kept on cutting.

"I think I hear something," Benton whispered, his ear

to the door. He tensed, then relaxed. "No. It was just someone walking by."

The next instant Fargo's hands were free. He made short work of the rope around his ankles.

"Give me a hand," Sergeant Petrie requested. He was still slicing at the rope around his wrists.

Instead, Fargo stood and moved to the weapons. A pile of gun belts caught his eye. He selected a Colt, checked that there were pills in the wheel, and shoved it into his holster. Only then did he turn and help Petrie. Together, they cut Private Benton free.

"At last," Benton said, rubbing his wrists. "But now what? There's three of us and a lot more of them."

"We have to save the people from the wagon train," Sergeant Petrie said. "We'll sneak out and over to the bluffs and cut them free."

"No," Fargo said.

About to stand, Sergeant Petrie stopped. "I beg your pardon?"

"There are too many. It'd take too long, and we'd be discovered." Fargo moved to the window and peered past the burlap.

The woman had finally stopped screaming, and would never scream again. Blackjack Tar was wiping his blood-smeared hands on her torn dress. The rest of the outlaws were admiring his handiwork.

"My orders are to save those people and that's exactly what I aim to do," Sergeant Petrie declared.

"You can't save them if you're dead," Fargo rebutted.

"What do you advise? We can't simply ride off and leave them."

"Who said anything about lighting a shuck?"

"Then what?" Petrie asked.

Fargo smiled grimly. "We kill every last one of these sons of bitches."

25

They armed themselves.

Fargo picked two more Colts and stuck them under his belt on either side of the buckle. He also chose a Spencer rifle.

So did Sergeant Petrie. He strapped on a holster with a Remington and a pocket pistol that he stuck in a pocket of his uniform.

Private Benton took a revolver that resembled his government-issue model, and a shotgun.

Fargo went to the window.

The outlaws were gathered around their fires. Bottles were being passed around. They were in good spirits, as well they should be.

Margaret's was the only sulky face in the bunch. Her arms were across her chest and she glared at the world and everyone in it.

Sergeant Petrie came to the window and peeked out the other side. "We can't drop all of them. They'll hunt cover and burn us out."

"Most likely," Fargo said.

"We can't rush them, either," Petrie said. "There's too much open ground. We might get half and then the rest would riddle us."

"Most likely," Fargo said again.

"I'm open to suggestions."

Fargo had been mulling it over. "The lean-to is to our

right. The other cabin is to our left. I'll make for the lean-to and you make for the other cabin and Benton will stay here. When I give a yell, we'll pour fire into them from three points. With any luck we'll get most of them before they get any of us. How does that strike you?"

"The trick will be to reach the lean-to and the other cabin unseen," Petrie said.

Fargo had been mulling that over, too. He motioned at the pile of clothes. "We'll disguise ourselves."

"Eh?" Sergeant Petrie looked, and smiled. "You without that bear coat and me without my uniform? Yes, it might work."

The pile contained all kinds of apparel. Homespun, store-bought, clothes a farmer would wear, clothes townsmen favored, shirts, pants, dresses, suits, jackets, and more.

Fargo traded his bearskin for a brown coat. He took off his own hat and put on a crumpled black one with a wide brim. Since his buckskin pants would give him away, he slid into a checkered pair that were a size too big.

Petrie shed his entire uniform. He put on clothes that were as close to those the outlaws were wearing as he could find.

"If we keep our heads down and move fast, they might not notice us," Fargo hoped.

Sergeant Petrie thrust out his hand. "In case we don't make it."

Fargo shook.

"How about me?" Private Benton nervously asked.

Petrie shook his hand, too.

Fargo opened the door a crack. None of the outlaws was looking in their direction. Blackjack Tar and Jacob Coarse were talking and chugging from bottles.

"I wish it was dark out," Petrie remarked.

"Not for hours yet," Fargo said. "We can't wait." He sucked in a deep breath. "I'll go first." Tucking his chin low, he pulled the black hat down over his eyes and slipped out. He expected a sharp cry and the blast of gunfire but nothing happened. When he came to the side of the cabin, he turned and walked to the back and then over toward the lean-to and the horses. He was tempted to look at the outlaws but didn't.

Acting casual, he went around the far end of the lean-to and then ran along it to the near end, close to the campfires. Hunkering, he pressed the Spencer to his shoulder.

Petrie had just reached the other cabin. He tried the door and stepped inside.

So far, so good, Fargo reflected.

There was a shout from the cabin Petrie had entered. A shot boomed, and another, and an outlaw lurched out with his hands to chest. He pointed at the cabin and tried to yell and collapsed.

For a few seconds the rest were frozen in surprise. A bellow from Blackjack brought them to their feet. Several started toward the cabin.

Fargo opened up. He shot at the ones rushing Petrie, saw gunsmoke spurt from the open door and knew Petrie was still alive.

Benton joined in.

The crossfire had a disconcerting effect on the outlaws. Some flattened. Some returned fire. Five were down when Blackjack roared for the rest to hunt cover. They scattered, firing as they ran.

A slug struck the lean-to above Fargo, and he instinctively ducked.

Lead poured from all directions.

At least one of the outlaws was a piss-poor shot; a horse whinnied stridently and crashed to the earth.

Fargo chose his targets carefully. He soon realized that numbers would tell, and the outlaws had the numbers. He spotted Jacob Coarse darting from one boulder to another and snapped a shot but missed.

At a shout from Blackjack Tar the firing from the other side stopped.

Fargo stopped shooting. Petrie and Benton banged off a few more shots, and they stopped, too.

In the silence, Blackjack Tar laughed. "This is what I get for not killing you bastards outright."

Fargo focused on a cluster of trees heavy with snow.

"You don't stand a prayer," Tar hollered. "Make it easy for us and I'll make it quick and clean for you. Come out with your hands in the air."

"Go to hell, mister," Private Benton yelled.

"The longer you hold out, the longer you'll take to die," Blackjack threatened.

Fargo saw movement in the trees and a patch of dark color. He fixed a bead and stroked the trigger.

An outlaw staggered into view, but it wasn't Tar. He reeled as if drunk, and collapsed.

A torrent of lead rained on the lead-to.

Flattening, Fargo was about to crab backward when a Sharps boomed loud and clear. From up high.

A figure was silhouetted on a bluff above the beehives. The figure whooped and raised an arm and waved, then dropped from sight before the outlaws could send a volley his way.

Jules Vallee, Fargo realized, and smiled. The old buzzard was still alive, and if he'd survived the avalanche, it could be that Josephine and Hortense had, too.

Private Benton began shooting and several outlaws responded in kind.

Fargo intended to work his way around the lean-to and hunt other cover. Skulking forms changed his mind. Three outlaws were over at the bluff, moving toward the beehive; in the lead was Jacob Coarse.

Fargo had a hunch what they were up to. Tar had sent them to bring captives to the trees. Tar would then threaten to kill the emigrants unless Fargo, and the troopers surrendered.

Like hell, Fargo thought, and moved to intercept them. The snow helped. On this side of the lean-to it was deep enough that if he stayed in a crouch, only part of his hat showed.

Coarse and the other two didn't spot him. They reached the first of the pockmarks and looked in. Coarse shook his head and they moved to the next. At a gesture from him, the pair entered and reappeared moments later with a woman. She had been tied and gagged but she could kick and buck and was doing her best to thwart them.

Coarse struck her with the butt of his rifle, a brutal blow to the temple that caused her to sag.

By then Fargo was close enough. He set the Spencer down and filled each hand with a Colt. As the pair was about to bear the woman off, he rose and simultaneously shot each man in the head.

Jacob Coarse turned and brought up his rifle.

Fargo shot him in the chest, both Colts at once. Coarse was slammed back but stayed on his feet. Fargo shot him again, in the gut, both Colts at once.

Coarse folded and clutched himself. "No!" he bleated.

"Yes," Fargo said, and triggered both Colts into his face.

Hurrying to the woman, Fargo scooped her into his arms and carried her into the pockmark. Four others were bound and gagged. Setting her down, he placed the Colts within easy reach, hiked his pant leg, and palmed the Arkansas toothpick. A few slashes and her arms and legs were free. He removed her gag, cradled her head, and lightly slapped first one cheek and then the other.

On the fourth slap she opened her eyes and looked wildly around. "Where? What?"

"You're safe," Fargo said. "I shot the men who were taking you." He quickly sat her up. "Listen. I don't have a lot of time." Reversing his grip on the toothpick, he pressed it to her hand. "Take this. Free as many as you can. Tell them to stay hid."

Blinking in confusion, the woman stammered, "Who are you? What's going on?"

"No time," Fargo said. "Do as I told you." Grabbing both Colts, Fargo reloaded and darted out. Shots blasted and hornets buzzed his ear.

Up on the cliff, Jules cut loose with his Sharps.

A man screamed.

By Fargo's reckoning ten or more of the outlaws were dead. There couldn't be more than half a dozen left, if that. Girding himself, he sprinted along the bluff. He weaved when a rifle muzzle was thrust out of the trees and spanged, and fired at the smoke.

Bending low, Fargo charged in. An outlaw—Buck—heaved upright. Fargo shot him. Another figure reared and Fargo spun and put slugs from both Colts into the figure's chest without realizing who it was.

Margaret Tar looked down at herself in disbelief, and collapsed.

Fargo took a few more bounds and a two-legged bear roared and hurtled at him. They fired at the same instant. Fargo felt a sting in his shoulder. He thumbed the hammers and stroked the triggers, thumbed and stroked, thumbed and stroked.

Blackjack Tar let out another roar. He rose onto the tips of his toes, his eyelids fluttering, then crashed to the snow with a thud, and convulsed.

Fargo went up, pressed both Colts to Tar's head, and fired a final time.

How long he stood there, he couldn't say. His ears were ringing and his shoulder was bleeding, but he was alive.

Suddenly so tired he could hardly stand, he walked out of the trees.

Sergeant Petrie and Private Benton had come out of the cabins. Petrie had been creased and Benton was limping.

"We did it, by God," Sergeant Petrie said.

Up on the cliff, Jules and Josephine and Hortense yelled and windmilled their arms.

"I need to find a bandage," Petrie said.

"I need a drink," Benton said.

Fargo knew what he needed. A week in Denver with a willing filly.

LOOKING FORWARD!
The following is the opening
section of the next novel in the exciting
***Trailsman* series from Signet:**

TRAILSMAN #379
HANGTOWN HELLCAT

Wyoming (Nebraska Territory), 1861—where a
dangerously beautiful woman entices Fargo into an
outlaw hellhole where honest men dance on air.

"We're in some deep soup, Fargo," said "Big Ed" Creighton, surveying the latest damage to his life's dream. "Back
in the rolling grass country we were making up to twelve
miles a day. Between twenty-two and twenty-five poles
per mile, slick as snot on a saddle horn. But I didn't take
the buffalo into account."

Creighton cursed under his breath and knocked the
dottle from his pipe on the heel of his boot.

"I'll have to send men back to set the poles again," he
said bitterly. "They were inferior wood to begin with, but
all we had. Most have been snapped—turned into scratch
poles for the blasted bison!"

The tall, lean, wide-shouldered man dressed in

buckskins said nothing to this tirade, merely removed his hat to shoo flies away with it. His calm, fathomless lake blue eyes stayed in constant motion, studying the surrounding slopes dotted with stands of juniper and scrub pine. From long habit as a scout, Skye Fargo watched for movement or reflection, not shapes.

"Two days before Independence Day," Creighton mused aloud, his tone almost wistful, "me and Charlie dug the first posthole in Julesburg, Colorado. Even with the nation plunging into war, President Lincoln himself took time to wish us luck. Think of it, Fargo! For the first time telegraphic dispatches will be sent from ocean to ocean."

Fargo did think about it and felt guilt lance into him deep. He glanced up into a storybook-perfect Western sky: ragged white parcels of cloud slid across a sky the pure blue color of a gas flame. The flat, endless horizon of eastern Wyoming was behind them, and now the magnificent, ermine-capped peaks of the Rockies—still called the Great Stony Mountains by the old trappers—surrounded them in majestic profusion.

And here's the fiddle-footed Trailsman, Fargo told himself, helping to blight it with a transcontinental telegraph that will only draw in settlements like flies to syrup. But at the time Creighton offered him fifty dollars a month to work as a scout and hunter, Fargo was light in the pockets and out of work.

All that was bad enough. But as Fargo read the obvious signs that Big Ed had missed, the words *pile on the agony* snapped in his mind like burning twigs.

"Buffalo!" Creighton spat out the word like a bad taste. "Fargo, we're already on a mighty tight schedule. My contract allows me a hundred and twenty days to link up with Jim Gamble's crew in Utah. If this keeps up, and we get trapped in a Wyoming winter . . ."

Creighton trailed off, for both men knew damn well what that would mean. Fargo had seen snow pile up so deep, and so long, in these parts that rabbits suffocated in their burrows. He recalled being caught in a blizzard just north of here that forced him to shelter inside a hollowed-out log for three days.

Stringing this line in late summer was travail enough, too. Mosquitoes all night, flies all day. Sometimes they drove men and beasts into frenzied fits. Trees to provide telegraph poles often had to be freighted great distances, as did the supplies needed to keep a virtual army of workers fed, clothed, and equipped.

And most vexing of all was the serious lack of drinking water. Fargo had spent more time locating water than he had hunting or scouting.

Now came this new trouble—Fargo studied the ground around the downed poles and felt a familiar foreboding. Instinct told him that, soon, lead would fly.

"Well," Creighton said, kicking at one of the broken poles, "wha'd'ya think? I could use the pocket relay and telegraph back to Fort Laramie. Maybe Colonel Langford could send enough soldiers to scatter the herds away from these parts."

Fargo shook his head. "The Laramie garrison has always been undermanned. And now half the troops have been ordered back east. That leaves just enough for force protection at the fort."

Creighton expelled a long, fluming sigh, nodding at the truth of Fargo's words. "Speak the truth and shame the devil. You got any suggestions?"

Fargo glanced at his employer. Big Ed Creighton, the son of penniless Irish immigrants, was a ruddy-complexioned, barrel-chested man in early middle age with a frank, weather-seamed face. He wore a broad-brimmed plainsman's hat, sturdy linsey trousers, and calfskin boots. He was the rain-maker for this ambitious project and a damn good man for the job, in Fargo's estimation. He rode every mile of this route before he mapped it out, and now he was working right alongside his men, eating the same food and taking the same risks.

One thing he was not, however, was a good reader of sign.

"Ed," Fargo said, "it's true that great shaggy brought down some poles back in the grassland. And we are sticking mostly to bottomland and valleys lately where you'll sometimes spot herds. But does the ground around us look like it's been torn up by sharp hooves?"

"Why . . ." Creighton surveyed the area around them. "Why, no. In fact, the grass isn't even flattened, is it?"

Fargo watched a skinny yellow coyote slink off through a nearby erosion gully. Clearly the boss did not like the turn this trail was taking.

"Then it must be Indians," Creighton said.

Fargo snorted. "I'd call that idea a bug of the genus hum. Sure, there's been Lakota and Cheyennes watching us like cats on a rat. They don't like what they see, and I don't blame them. But they don't understand what we're up to, and when the red man doesn't understand something he tends to wade in slow. Everything connected to the white man is likely to be bad medicine—they aren't touching those poles. Not yet, anyhow."

Creighton looked like a man who had woken up in the wrong year. The weather grooves in his face deepened when he frowned. "You yourself are always pointing out how the Indians are notional and unpredictable. Back in western Missouri, the Fox tribe learned how to use stolen crowbars to rip up railroad tracks."

Fargo sighed patiently. "Indian scares" were common

because they stirred up settlers. Stirred-up settlers meant more soldiers and thus, more lucrative contracts to the Eastern opportunists supplying them.

"Ed, if it was Indians who tore down these poles, then their horses have iron-shod hooves."

These words struck Creighton like a bolt out of the blue. He hung fire for a few seconds, not understanding. "You're saying white men did this?"

"'Pears so."

"But . . . Fargo, there's nary a settlement anywhere near here. *What* white men?"

"That's got me treed," Fargo admitted. "But there were three of them, and they rode out headed due south. Buckshot left at sunup going after game. He should be back anytime now. We'll pick up that trail and see where it takes us."

"White men," Creighton repeated as the men headed toward the two mounts calmly taking off the grass nearby. "Why would white men go to such trouble to sabotage a telegraph line?"

Fargo forked leather and reined his Ovaro around to the west, pressuring him to a trot with his knees.

"Because," he suggested, "the telegraph is even faster than a posse. There's been strikes against bull trains and mail carriers in this neck of the woods. Even a few kidnappings of stagecoach passengers on the Overland route. Good chance the owlhoot gang behind those crimes don't want that telegraph going through. Back east, the talking wires have put the kibosh on plenty of road agents."

"All that rings right enough," Creighton agreed reluctantly, gigging his blaze-faced sorrel up beside Fargo's black-and-white stallion.

"It does and it doesn't," Fargo hedged, keeping a weather eye out and loosening his sixteen-shot Henry repeater in its saddle scabbard. "Most outlaws are a lazy tribe with damn poor trailcraft. They like good meals, saloons, and beds with a whore in them. You'll most often find them in towns, not running all over Robin Hood's barn. Like you said, there's no settlements around here."

"Right now," Creighton said, "Jim Gamble and his Pacific crew are racing to beat us to Fort Bridger. Working in those God-forgotten deserts of Nevada and Utah. Black cinder mountains, alkali dust, and warpath Paiutes—until now, I figured we had the easy part."

"You might be building a pimple into a peak," Fargo reminded him despite his own growing sense of unease. "If it's just three outlaws, me and Buckshot will salt their tails. That sort of work is right down our alley."

"You two are just the boys to do it," Creighton agreed. "It's *water* I'm really fretting about. I'll tell you who will soon get rich out west—well diggers and men who build windmills to drive the water. You won't find one in a nickel novel, but one man with a steam drill is worth a shithouse full of gunslingers."

"I respect honest labor, Ed, but to hell with wells and windmills."

Creighton flashed a grin through the dusty patina on his face. "To hell with this magnetic telegraph too, huh?"

Fargo grinned back. "I'm straddling the fence on that one," he admitted. "Couriers and express riders are murdered every day, including some good friends of mine. It's an ill Chinook that doesn't blow *some*body some good, I reckon."

By now the two men had ridden into sight of the main work crew. Under the watchful eye of Taffy Blackford, the Welsh foreman, workers were busy digging postholes, setting and shaping poles, and stringing wire. Other men had scattered out to scavenge wood for poles. A carpenter was at work repairing the broken tongue of a wagon.

"Here comes Buckshot now," Fargo remarked, spotting a rider approaching them on a grulla, an Indian-broke bluish gray mustang also known as a smoky. "Something must be on the spit. He rode out without eating and he's always hungry as a field hand when he gets back. He'd ought to be feeding his face right about now."

Buckshot Brady had been hired at Fargo's insistence. He was an ace Indian tracker and experienced frontiersman who had learned his lore at the side of Kit Carson and Uncle Dick Wootton during the shining times at Taos. He earned his name from carrying a sawed-off double ten in a special-rigged swivel sling on his right hip.

Buckshot loped closer and Fargo saw that his face was grim as an undertaker's.

"Trouble, old son?" Fargo greeted him.

"Skye," Buckshot replied quietly, drawing rein, "I got me a God-fear."

The hair on Fargo's nape instantly stiffened. Buckshot's famous "God-fears" were as reliable as the equinox.

"Ed," Fargo snapped, tugging his brass-framed Henry from its boot, "whistle the men to cover."

"What's—?"

"Now!" Fargo ordered and Creighton reached for the silver whistle on its chain beneath his collar.

Just then, however, a hammering racket of gunfire erupted from the boulder-strewn slope on their left. Fargo watched, his blood icing, as a rope of blood spurted from one side of the carpenter's head and he folded to the ground like an empty gunnysack.

"God-in-whirlwinds!" a shocked Ed Creighton exclaimed.

An eyeblink later, the withering volley of lead shifted to the three men, and Creighton, too, crashed to the ground, trapped under his dying horse.

NEW IN HARDCOVER

THE LAST OUTLAWS
The Lives and Legends of Butch Cassidy and the Sundance Kid

by Thom Hatch

Butch Cassidy and the Sundance Kid are two of the most celebrated figures of American lore. As leaders of the Wild Bunch, also known as the Hole-in-the-Wall Gang, they planned and executed the most daring bank and train robberies of the day, with an uprecedented professionalism.

The Last Outlaws brilliantly brings to life these thrilling, larger-than-life personalities like never before, placing the legend of Butch and Sundance in the context of a changing—and shrinking—American West, as the rise of 20th century technology brought an end to a remarkable era. Drawing on a wealth of fresh research, Thom Hatch pushes aside the myth and offers up a compelling, fresh look at these icons of the Wild West.

**Available wherever books are sold or at
penguin.com**